FRIGHTEN

"It's all right, now. Calm yourself. That's it. Now, stand up." He pulled her to her feet. "Look me in the eyes."

Vicky shrank away. Something was not right. "Darren?" she said. "Darren, is that you?"

"Hush!" There was an unmistakable harshness to the whispered voice. "And do as you're told. Look me in the eyes, I said."

"No, no!" Vicky cried out, and she struggled to pull herself free from the gripping hands, which had turned hot and hard. "Let go of me!" she shrieked. She turned away. "Let me go…!"

Also by Paul Stewart

The Hanging Tree

FRIGHT TRAIN

Paul Stewart

■SCHOLASTIC

Scholastic Children's Books,
Commonwealth House, 1-19 New Oxford Street,
London WC1A 1NU, UK
a division of Scholastic Ltd
London ~ New York ~ Toronto ~ Sydney ~ Auckland
Mexico City ~ New Delhi ~ Hong Kong

First published in the UK by Scholastic Ltd, 2001

Text copyright © Paul Stewart, 2001

ISBN 0 439 99871 9

Typeset by
Cambrian Typesetters, Frimley, Camberley, Surrey
Printed by Cox and Wyman Ltd, Reading, Berks.

10 9 8 7 6 5 4 3 2 1

For Joseph

1

"I told you we should have left earlier!" said Vicky impatiently, as she stared out of the window. A water main had burst in the high street up ahead and their bus was in the middle of a huge traffic jam. It hadn't moved more than a dozen metres in the last five minutes. "If we miss that train, I'll... I'll..."

"We won't," said Darren, and squeezed her hand. "Trust me!"

Vicky bit her tongue. It was Darren's laid-back attitude to life that had attracted her to him in the first place. Now she was beginning to wish she was going out with someone a little more uptight – someone who would have allowed more than half an hour to get to the station.

"Tell you what," said Darren. "If we haven't moved in the next five minutes, we'll get off and walk. It's not that far now."

Vicky promptly jumped to her feet. "Then why wait five minutes?" she said. "Come on!"

Darren smiled. He knew how important the holiday was to her. After a gruelling autumn term at college – and an even more gruelling evening job in a restaurant to pay for it – Vicky had talked about nothing else for the previous week. Every evening she would pore over the details of the cottage they'd booked.

"It's going to be fantastic!" she'd told him. "Log fires at night. Long walks during the day – maybe even some cross-country skiing if the weather forecast is right. And I've got a little surprise in store," she added.

And Darren had laughed, and pointed out the even better news, that there was a pub right next door to the cottage.

"Which solves the problem of Christmas dinner!" Vicky had said. "Oh, Darren! Our first time away from home at Christmas ... I can't wait!"

Darren followed Vicky as she marched down the stairs of the bus, grabbed her rucksack from the luggage area and asked the driver to let them off. He grabbed his own rucksack and swung it on to his back. The bus doors opened with a hiss.

"Cheers, mate," said Darren, as he stepped down on to the pavement.

"Which way?" said Vicky urgently, her breath like puffs of cloud in the cold late-afternoon air.

Darren pointed ahead. "Down there, and then..."

But Vicky was already gone, striding purposefully ahead, past shops decorated with Santas and reindeer and bright, coloured lights on one side, and the line of motionless cars on the other. Darren trotted after her, taking care not to slip on the freezing scraps of leaves.

"Left here," he said. "Then right."

A while later, Vicky saw the grand Victorian entrance to the station at the far end of the road. She glanced at her watch, squawked with horror and broke into a shuffling run. The heavy rucksack swayed from side to side.

"It's all right," Darren said. "We've got eight minutes."

"*Three* minutes!" Vicky panted.

"But I make it 5.27," said Darren. "The train leaves at..."

"At 5.30!" said Vicky. She wiped her brow on her sleeve. Despite the cold, she was wet with sweat.

"But I thought..."

"Oh, stop talking!" Vicky shouted breathlessly. "Let's ... just ... get there..."

As they emerged, puffing and panting, into the

station concourse, the clock above the departures board clicked to 5.29.

"Platform?" Vicky cried. "Which platform?"

Darren scanned the board. "Edinburgh, Wick..." he read off. "Number 11. Come on!"

Barging their way through the milling crowds of people, Vicky and Darren hurried towards the platform. The seconds ticked past.

"Excuse me," Vicky shouted at a couple with backpacks looking even more lost than they were. "Excu... Get out of my way!" She shoved them aside. Darren followed her through the gap.

"Oi!" the man yelled after them.

"Sorry," Darren called back, for Vicky. "Our train's about to leave."

The man dumped his bag on the ground and, with fists clenched, started towards him. He was big and heavy; he looked mean. "I've a good mind..."

Darren raised his hands defensively as he backed away. "I said we were sorry, mate," he said. "It was an accident."

"Leave it, Baz," said his girlfriend, grabbing his arm. "We don't want any trouble. Not now... Anyway, *our* train's just about to leave too!"

The man glared at Darren for a moment longer, before relaxing his shoulders and turning away. "If you're sure you're OK, Shel," he said to the girl.

"I'm fine," she nodded. "Just find the platform we need."

Darren hurried after Vicky. It wasn't the first time that her volatile temper had almost landed them – or rather, *him* – in trouble.

"You'd better watch it in future!" the man yelled after him.

"Come *on*!" shouted Vicky, up ahead.

Darren sighed and quickened his pace. Platform 11 was ahead of them now, and the train was still there. But not for much longer. A station guard was standing on the platform at the middle of the train, arm raised, whistle in his mouth.

"Wait!" shouted Vicky. She hurtled past the ticket collector at the gate and on along the platform. The guard glanced at his watch. "Please!" she screamed.

With a last-minute sprint, Darren got to the first door in the train before Vicky. He pulled it open and leapt on board. Vicky – red-faced and gasping for air – arrived a few seconds later. Darren pulled her up the steps, slammed the door shut and leaned back out of the window.

The guard lowered his arm, blew his whistle, and the train glided smoothly away. Vicky swung the heavy rucksack down from her shoulders.

"Thank heavens for that!" she gasped. "We made it!"

Darren pulled the window up and turned to her. "See?" he said, and grinned. "I told you to trust me!"

Vicky ignored him. "So, where do we sit then?" she said, and peered into the carriage. It was almost full, and the few empty seats there were had reservation tickets sticking out of the headrests. She tutted irritably. "I knew we should have booked seats when we got the tickets," she said.

Darren shrugged. "We saved a tenner," he said. "Typical that the railway company we choose should be the only one to charge a booking fee."

"Yes, but we can't stand the whole way," Vicky protested. "It's over eight hundred kilometres away!"

Darren turned and pressed the button to the carriage behind them – the rear carriage on the train. The electric door slid smoothly open, to reveal a plush buffet car on the other side. Darren grinned. "Very nice," he said, stepping inside.

Even Vicky couldn't resist a smile. "OK," she said. "Maybe I'll let you off this time, after all."

Like the rest of the train, the buffet car was brand new. The floor was covered with a thick grey carpet with yellow and blue chevrons, the seats were upholstered in a grey and blue checked material, while the curved rails and hand-holds were covered in a new non-slip dimpled plastic. Everything was bright, clean and airy – and there wasn't a trace of graffiti to be seen.

"Looks like Network Railways have been splashing out," Vicky commented.

"So they should," Darren grumbled. "The profits they make!"

They stowed their rucksacks at the top of the stacked luggage compartment to their left, and headed up the aisle. On either side of them, two-person bench-seats faced one another, separated by laminated tables – five down the left-hand side, four down the right. And there was more seating at the far end of the carriage, where curved wall-benches and high tables formed a snack-and-chat area opposite the buffet counter.

Although the carriage was practically empty, most of the four-seat compartments had been taken up by a single passenger, who had spread out their belongings in an attempt to deter anyone sitting either beside or opposite them. At the far end, a man was leaning against the counter of the closed buffet reading his newspaper.

Vicky homed in on an empty table, halfway down the aisle on her left, and sat with her back to the engine. Darren slid in opposite her.

"Perfect," he said. "Scotland, here we come!"

Vicky smiled. Now that they were finally seated on the moving train, she could allow herself to unwind. She leant forwards and clutched Darren's hands in her own. "Love you," she whispered.

"Love you, too," he mouthed back, embarrassed that someone might hear. With the wheels all but silent on the track and no one else in the carriage talking, their whispers seemed to echo. He turned and looked back at the buffet. The steel roller was still down. "I'm famished," he said. "I wish they'd hurry up and open it."

"Do you fancy a sandwich?" said Vicky. She reached into her shoulder bag. "There's pilchard and ketchup, pilchard and pickle or pilchard and curry paste."

Darren pulled a face. "Anything without pilchard?" he said.

"It was all we had left," said Vicky.

"Yeah, well, like I said, I wish they'd hurry up and open the buffet." He looked at his watch, then turned and looked at the closed steel roller, eyes narrowed – as if glaring at them would make them magically spring open.

"Be patient!" said Vicky.

Darren snorted. "Patient? You can talk! You nearly got me beaten up back there."

"Beaten up?"

"You knocked into Shel," said Darren, "and big Baz didn't like it!"

Vicky shook her head. "I don't know what you're talking about," she said. "All I know is, if it hadn't been for me, we'd have missed the train."

Darren opened his mouth, then closed it again. She had a point. "I'm glad we won't be coming back to our old house," he said, deliberately changing the subject.

Vicky glanced out of the window. They'd left the big city buildings behind now, and were speeding through a landscape of suburban semis, each one with a twinkling Christmas tree in its window.

She turned to look at Darren. "I don't know, I think I'm really going to miss that place."

"I know," said Darren. "But think of the place we'll be moving into when we get back. Gas. Electricity. Hot and cold water. A shower! I can hardly wait!"

"I know, but..." said Vicky quietly. "It was just so beautiful where we were."

The pair of them had been squatting in a grand, if disconnected, house in an opulent mews for almost a year when the official letters started to arrive asking – then demanding – that they leave. They'd have been kicked out a lot sooner if Elena in the basement hadn't been studying law. She'd made it her business to bone up on all the legal loopholes that might delay their final eviction.

"I bet we'll never live anywhere that grand again," she said glumly.

"Maybe not," said Darren. "But at least in the new place we won't have to flush the toilet with a bucket. A new year. A new beginning. The trouble with you, Vicky Amis, is you don't like change. It's going to be fine. It's going to be fantastic! Trust me."

"I *do* trust you, Darren," she said softly.

Darren blushed and winced and looked round awkwardly. None of the other passengers returned his gaze, but he knew they must have heard. He cleared his throat. "The buffet's still shut," he said.

Vicky laughed. "The trouble with *you*, Darren Roberts, is you get embarrassed too easily." She turned and looked longingly at the steel roller still down over the buffet counter. "I could murder a bacon butty!"

An hour later, the buffet was still closed. What was more, there were none of the mouth-watering smells that might have been expected if its opening was imminent. No brewing coffee. No grilling bacon. No toasting bread. Vicky and Darren weren't the only ones getting impatient.

A tall, heavily built man with thick dark hair, cut very short, began hammering on the steel roller with his fist.

"Open up!" he bellowed. "I demand some service."

He moved round to the side-door marked *Private* which led to the area behind the buffet-bar, and hammered even louder.

"Come on!" he roared. "I can hear you're in there."

Darren looked at Vicky and winked. "Action Man's losing it," he said.

"The Ocelot doesn't seem any too chuffed

either," Vicky giggled, as a woman in a fur coat muttered angrily under her breath in Spanish.

Without knowing a single thing about any of them, Darren and Vicky had given nicknames to all their fellow passengers and, sniggering with amusement, furtively whispered life histories to go with them. Apart from Action Man and the soprano Ocelot, there were three others: the Spiv, a sharp-suited, gel-quiffed wheeler-dealer with a mobile phone and a neverending supply of nicotine gum; Matron, a roly-poly, rosy-cheeked, lacy dumpling of a granny who smelled of flowery perfume; and the Starlet, a bottle-blonde bodybuilder in lycra and fleece.

Action Man was back at the steel roller. "Open up!" he was shouting. "Open up, now!" He sounded posh, just as Vicky and Darren had known he would.

"Bet he plays rugby as well," said Darren.

"Yeah, and has weekends away with the Territorial Army," said Vicky scornfully.

"Still, at least he's trying to get the buffet open," said Darren. "No one else is – and I'm starving!"

Vicky rummaged through her bag and pulled out the plastic box full of the assorted pilchard sandwiches. She held them out. Darren turned his nose up.

"Not *that* starving," he said.

Vicky laughed, slipped her trainers off and put her feet up on Darren's lap. She glanced out of the window, but the lighting inside the carriage was so bright that all she saw was the buffet car itself, reflected back. She leant across and pressed her face to the glass.

"What can you see?" said Darren.

"Not much," said Vicky. "Fields, trees. The odd street lamp. A car... Blimey, we are going fast!" she exclaimed.

"Good," said Darren. He stood up, rounded the table and slipped in next to Vicky. He put his arm around her shoulder and squeezed. "The faster we go, the quicker we get there."

At the back of the carriage, Action Man had stopped his hammering and was leaning against one of the high tables, staring furiously ahead. The Ocelot was pouting into a vanity mirror and poking at her mouth with carmine-red lipstick. The Starlet had her Walkman on; her eyes were closed but her feet were tapping. The Spiv – mobile to his ear – was pacing to and fro and speaking in a hushed, urgent voice, while Matron was rummaging through a large cellophane bag full of extra-strong mints.

Vicky leant round and whispered into Darren's ear. "Just imagine," she said, her eyes flitting round the hotchpotch of passengers. "Everyone in the whole world dies except the people in this carriage. Between us we have to repopulate the planet."

Darren spluttered with horror and pulled away. "You what?" he exclaimed. The Ocelot glanced up from her mirror and eyed him disapprovingly. Matron muttered something under her breath.

"It was just a thought," Vicky laughed.

"No, it wasn't," Darren chuckled. "It was a nightmare. An absolute nightm—"

At that moment there was a sudden judder, followed by the deafening squeal of metal on metal. Darren and Vicky were thrown forwards across the table, then back into the bench-seat – then forwards again, harder than ever. All round them, the sound of screaming filled the air.

Darren braced his legs against the seat opposite and fumbled for Vicky's hand. She grasped it gratefully. They closed their eyes. They gritted their teeth and—

CRASH!

It felt as if a wrecking-ball had smashed into the side of the carriage. Those lucky enough to be sitting at the moment of impact clung on for grim death, while those standing were tossed to the ground like limp puppets. Luggage flew down from the racks. Glass shattered. Metal buckled. The brakes wailed like banshees. Yet the train did not slow down.

"Oh, Darren!" Vicky cried out.

"Hold on!" said Darren, clasping her tightly. "Just hold on."

Just then, a dazzling flash lit up the carriage, followed by complete darkness as the lights all went out at once. Now that they were unable to see, it no longer felt as though they were speeding along a track, but rather tumbling headlong into a bottomless pit.

Down, down, down, they fell. The air roared. The passengers screamed.

"Darren!" cried Vicky. "Where are you?"

"H... Here," came a trembling voice.

"Where?" said Vicky desperately. She fumbled all about her: round the table, the floor beneath, the seat beside her where, only moments earlier, Darren had been sitting. "Darren!" She sounded hysterical now. "Darren, I can't find you!"

The darkness was impenetrable – an absolute suffocating blackness she could not grow accustomed to, that seemed to dance before her eyes. Deep, muffled voices, groaning with pain and gibbering with fear echoed all round. The air smelled of scorched metal and smouldering electric circuitry.

Overwhelmed by a terrible dread, Vicky gripped the armrest. She felt giddy, sick. Her heart hammered, her breath came in short, fitful gasps. The train gave another colossal jolt and she was thrown out of her seat and into the aisle.

"Darren?" she wailed, as she pulled herself up on to her knees. Scalding tears coursed down her face. "Darren, answer me ... if you can," she sniffed. "Please, Darren. Please..."

And then she found him – or rather, he found her. She felt his hands take hold of her own and heard his voice, soothing, lulling.

"It's all right, now. Calm yourself. That's it. Now, stand up." He pulled her to her feet. "Look me in the eyes."

Vicky shrank away. Something was not right. "Darren?" she said. "Darren, is that you?"

"Hush!" There was an unmistakable harshness to the whispered voice. "And do as you're told. Look me in the eyes, I said."

"No, no!" Vicky cried out, and she struggled to pull herself free from the gripping hands, which had turned hot and hard. "Let go of me!" she shrieked. She turned away. "Let me go!"

But the person, whoever it was, would not let go. Talon-like nails dug into the soft flesh of her forearm.

"Now, now, Michelle," it chided, "it's a little too late for all that, isn't it?" the soft voice told her.

"But ... but, I'm not Mi—"

"LOOK!" screamed the voice, and the two hands clamped themselves to either side of her head and wrenched it round.

Trembling with fear, Vicky opened her eyes. She gasped. In front of her were two slivers of red light, glinting like cat's eyes from the dark. As she stared, they came closer – growing larger, brighter. The smell of burnt flesh made her nose quiver. The red eyes came closer still. They seemed to be boring right inside her head.

"It's pointless trying to resist, Michelle," came the voice, and Vicky heard a gleeful chorus of cackling and whooping. "You belong here now."

Like a rabbit, dazzled by the full-beam of oncoming headlamps, Vicky stared back, motionless, frozen, unable even to blink. Why did he keep calling her Michelle? What was going on? And where *was* Darren?

"Darren!" she screamed. "Help me! Hel—"

All at once, there was a second crash, so deafeningly violent it made the first collision seem like a mere judder. It ripped through the carriage like an explosion. The floor shook. The air itself splintered into a million jagged pieces and fell away like shattered glass. Vicky was tossed backwards like a rag doll.

The next instant, there was a screech of metal and the train came to an abrupt standstill. The lights flickered and came on, dimmer than before, but bright enough to see by. Vicky opened her eyes. She was sprawled out on the seat across the aisle. She pulled herself up, looked round – and shivered with fear.

There were bodies all round her; bleeding, broken bodies, draped over the wreckage of twisted metal. A pair of trainers were sticking out from beneath the twisted seat in front of her. Familiar colours. A familiar swoosh...

"Darren," Vicky gasped. "*Darren!*"

2

In all, the crash couldn't have lasted more than a few seconds. To Vicky, however, it seemed an eternity. And even now, as she dropped to her knees beside Darren – who had fallen and slipped, and was now trapped beneath the seat – it was as though time hadn't yet cranked itself up to normal speed. Her hands moved to his face impossibly slowly and when she spoke, her voice came slow and deep.

"Speak to me!" it boomed. She knelt next to him and lay her head on the carpet, ear down, staring into his face. "Say something!"

For a moment there was nothing. Then suddenly, time speeded up once again. Darren's eyelids flickered. Vicky stroked his cheek gently with her fingertips. The eyes snapped open abruptly and stared all round, wild and unseeing.

"It's all right, angel," said Vicky, her voice its normal pitch.

"Vicky," Darren groaned. "Oh, God, it was awful, awful…"

"I know," said Vicky. She wrapped her arms around his neck and hugged tightly. "But it's all right now," she said, the way her mum had comforted her when, as a girl, she had woken up from nightmares, sweating and confused. "It's over now." She frowned. "Can you move?"

Darren nodded. "I think so," he said. "I…" He tugged at his leg. "My trousers are caught."

Vicky slid under the seat to inspect. A broken spring had snagged itself on his army fatigues. "Just stay still," she said, as she pulled the knot of material free, taking care not to tear it. "There, you're free now."

She stood up and helped him to wriggle out from beneath the seat. Darren looked up. "Wh… What happened?" he asked numbly.

"We crashed, I guess," said Vicky, weakly. Her face crumpled, and tears began to stream down her cheeks. "But we're all right," she said. "We survived, Darren. We're alive!"

All round them, Vicky's words were being repeated as the strangers – strangers no longer – helped one another to their feet, then to their seats, and offered each other handkerchiefs, sweet tea from vacuum flasks, kind words, explanations...

Vicky listened in disbelief. How could the other passengers be talking when they had looked so lifeless just a moment before?

"Are you two all right?" came a voice. She looked up. It was Action Man. Apart from looking a little dishevelled, he seemed fine – no cuts, no bruises, no broken bones.

"I... We're all right," she heard Darren replying.

The pair of them climbed to their feet. Vicky looked around her in dazed confusion. Nobody was injured. No damage had been done. Even the windows were intact – despite the terrible sound of smashing glass she'd heard. Her pale reflection stared back at her, looking frightened and confused.

"Terrible!" the Ocelot was screeching behind her. "Absolutely terrible."

Vicky turned to Darren.

"I... I don't understand," she whispered.

"We must have hit another train," said Darren.

"Unless some bloody kids put a rock on the tracks," said Action Man.

"Or a tray!" added the Starlet indignantly. "I read about it in the papers. One steel tray can derail a whole train."

"A tray!" the Ocelot cried. "What kind of country is this?"

"They want to lock them up so they do," said

Matron, as she bustled round collecting the extra-strong mints which were strewn all over the carpet.

"Too right!" the Spiv chipped in. "For a moment back there, I thought I was a goner. Honest, I did!"

"The worst experience of my entire life!" said Matron.

Vicky sat down on her seat and pulled Darren in beside her. She turned to him anxiously. "What ... what did you actually see?"

"See?" he said. "I couldn't see anything. The lights all went out."

"Yes, but ... I..." She burst into tears.

"Hey, Vicky," said Darren, hugging her tightly. "It's all right now. We've had an accident. But we're OK!"

"I... I know," Vicky sobbed. "It's just... Oh, Darren. I heard voices. Horrible voices. Shouting. Sneering. And I felt these hands gripping hold of me really tight, and these eyes..."

"Vicky, Vicky," said Darren softly. He nuzzled into her neck. "You're in shock." He looked round at Matron. "Is there any more of that sweet tea going?" he asked.

The old woman nodded warmly and started rummaging in her large bag.

"And ... and then," Vicky said, sniffing and wiping her eyes, "when the lights first came back on ... it wasn't like this!" She swept her arm round in a wide arc. "Bit of a mess and nothing more!"

"Sssh!" said Darren, wiping a tear from the tip of her nose with his finger.

"But it wasn't," she whispered urgently. "It was all wreckage. And, and..." The tears welled up again. "Bodies, Darren. *Dead* bodies."

"Here we are, my dear," came a voice. It was Matron. She held out the plastic cup full of steaming tea. "Nice and sweet," she said.

"Thanks," said Vicky. She reached out, clutched it with two shaking hands and brought it to her lips.

"Nice?" said Darren.

Vicky pulled a face. "I hate sugar in tea," she said.

"You drink it all up," said Matron. "It'll do you good." She turned away, flask raised high. "Any more for any more?" she said.

The moment she was gone, Vicky turned back to Darren. "It kept calling me Michelle," she said.

Darren frowned. "What did?"

"The voice I heard. Michelle this, Michelle that..."

Her hands were shaking so much she spilt some of the tea down her front. Darren took the cup from her and placed it on the table.

"You know what I think?" he said.

"What?" said Vicky. She wiped her eyes again.

"I think you were knocked out," he said. He

looked round. "Maybe the Ocelot's vanity box hit you."

"But..." said Vicky, feeling all over head. "Surely there'd be a bump."

"Whiplash, then," said Darren. "When the brakes went on. That can make you pass out."

"But..." said Vicky again.

"Hearing voices, seeing lights," said Darren. "You were unconscious – just for a moment."

"But it was so real!" said Vicky.

"Nightmares are," said Darren. "They kind of borrow from real life and jumble everything up. That's why you heard the name Michelle."

"It is?"

"Course it is. I was telling you about Shel earlier on, do you remember? The girl you knocked into in the station." He snorted. "You were probably imagining it was big Baz beating you up."

"I was?" said Vicky weakly. She looked at Darren, her brow furrowed with anxiety. "Are you sure?" she said.

Darren shrugged. "It makes sense to me."

"But what about the train wreckage?" she said. "The dead bodies?"

"What *about* them?" he said. "You were in a train crash. It was just more of the same nightmare." He smiled and gripped her hands. Vicky flinched. "Why don't you finish your tea?" he said.

Vicky smiled back bravely. Everything Darren

had said made perfect sense. And yet... It was like no nightmare she'd ever had before. The hard, burning grip of those bony fingers pinching into her wrists had felt so real... And anyway, she wondered, was it even possible to have nightmares when you were unconscious? Apparently it was. The evidence in front of her now was incontrovertible. The train was not a wreck. The passengers were not dead. Thank God! She drank the sweet tea down in one sickly gulp and turned back to Darren.

"Maybe it would've been better if we'd missed the train after all," she said.

"You won't be saying that when we get to Scotland," said Darren.

"*If* we get there," said Vicky gloomily. "We're still not even moving."

"We will," Darren assured her. "And this time tomorrow we'll be sprawled out on a rug in front of a roaring fire." He looked round and saw the Spiv with his face pressed to his cupped hands at the window. "Can you see anything, mate?"

"Nah," said the Spiv. "It's pitch-black out there."

"Terrible. Terrible," the Ocelot was still muttering, despite the consoling words from Matron.

"It's all right, dear," she was saying. "Just calm yourself."

Vicky looked up to see Action Man closing in on the Starlet.

"You're OK then?" he said.

"Yeah, f ... fine," came the shaken reply.

"The name's Greg, by the way," he boomed. "Greg Tolson. How do you do?"

The Starlet giggled. "Hi, Greg," she said. "I'm Amanda. Amanda Hurley. My friends call me Mandy."

"Mandy it is, then," said Greg.

Vicky smiled wryly. It amused her the way that people would sit together in absolute silence unless some accident or misfortune gave them the excuse to communicate with one another. Then there was no stopping them.

Behind her, Matron had also decided to abandon her anonymity.

"Evelyn Grange," she announced, and held out her hand.

The Ocelot shook it limply. "Maria Fernandez," she said. "Most charmed, I'm sure." She retrieved her hand. "How long do you think we will be stuck here?"

"Heaven knows," said Miss Grange. "And I've got people meeting me," she said.

"I, too," said Maria Fernandez impatiently. "It is all too, too inconvenient." It hadn't taken long for her relief to give way to irritation, Vicky noted, and sighed. If first impressions were anything to go by, then she knew she wanted nothing at all to do with Maria Fernandez. She turned her attention back to the couple up by the shuttered buffet.

"And what's taking you all the way up to Scotland?" Greg was asking. "Assuming we ever get there."

"An athletics event," came the reply.

"I suspected as much," said Greg. "With a body as fit as yours, I knew you had to be into sports. What do you do? High jump? Hundred metres?"

"Hurdles," she said.

Greg grinned. "Hurdling Hurley, eh? Great stuff! Course, where I really shine is in the javelin department," he said, and winked.

Mandy giggled and punched him on the arm. "Gre-eg!" she said with mock outrage.

"What? What did I say?" said Greg. He laughed. "Actually, rugger's more my game..."

Vicky nudged Darren in the side with her elbow. "He *does* play rugby," she said.

"Never doubted it for a minute," said Darren. He nodded up at the Spiv. "I'm Darren and this is Vicky," he said.

"Hi, Simon Droy," said Simon as he flicked his fringe back and leaned forwards to shake Vicky's hand. She flinched again, drew away and then, aware that she might have appeared rude, glanced down at her watch.

"Blast!"

"What?" said Darren.

Vicky shook her wrist and looked at the watch again. The glass was cracked. "It must be broken," she said. "It's stuck on 18.42."

Darren looked at his own watch. It too had stopped, the hands fixed at just gone twenty-to-seven. "So there's no way of knowing how long we've been stuck here already."

Vicky looked back out through the window. The darkness was as impenetrable as before, and oddly menacing. It was like staring into the black pupil of some monstrous eye.

"Not that we're in any great rush," Darren was saying. "It doesn't really matter what time we get there."

"Lucky you," said Simon, his voice thin and petulant. "Someone's meant to be meeting me off the train with me ticket," he said. He pulled out his mobile and tapped at the numbers.

"Ticket?" said Darren.

"For the Scotland-Estonia qualifying match," he said. He shook his mobile irritably. "I can't seem to get a line..." He dialled again and bellowed down the mouthpiece. "Hello? Hello? This is Simon Droy. I... Nothing!" he muttered, as he slammed the aerial down and shoved the phone into his jacket pocket. "Piece of junk!"

"I think we might be in a tunnel," said Vicky.

"Yeah, well," said Simon. "If I miss the match

because of all this I'm going to sue Network Railways. I've done it before," he added.

"Did you win?" said Darren.

Simon Droy smirked. "Natch," he said. His nasal voice twanged gleefully. "I always do."

Darren nodded, and he and Vicky exchanged glances. That type always did!

"I do wish they'd make some kind of official announcement," Maria Fernandez was saying. "Surely someone must know what happened."

"I agree," said Miss Grange. "It's the not knowing what exactly is going on that's so awful. I mean, it's wonderful that we're all in one piece, but..."

Vicky turned to them. "Do either of you have the right time?" she asked.

Miss Grange looked at her watch and tutted. "It seems to have stopped," she said.

"So has mine," Maria Fernandez said. "I must have knocked it when we crashed." She breathed out impatiently. "My husband is going to be so concerned if I'm delayed."

"So will my cousin Clarissa," said Miss Grange. "Dreadful worrier at the best of times, she is." She looked round her. "Oh, why doesn't somebody tell us what's going on?"

Vicky turned away. Simon Droy, glistening with sweat, was once again stabbing furiously at his mobile. Behind her, Greg Tolson was complaining loudly about the appalling state of the railways and how, if it hadn't been for the idiot who'd scratched his Porsche, he wouldn't be travelling by train now. Miss Grange and Maria Fernandez became more and more shrill.

"It's disgraceful!" said Miss Grange.

"Outrageous!" agreed Maria Fernandez.

Greg had begun hammering on the steel roller at the buffet again. Mandy joined in.

"Hello? Hello!" Simon Droy yelled into his phone.

Vicky looked at Darren and smiled wryly. "This is fun, isn't it?" she said.

Darren laughed. "They'll get us moving again soon," he said. "Once they've re-jigged the signals—"

Just then, the train gave a jolt and lurched forwards. As one, the passengers fell silent and held their breath. The train abruptly ground to a halt. A groan filled the air. Then it started up again – more smoothly this time – and kept going.

Suddenly, everyone was looking at everyone else and smiling. Although the train was moving painfully slowly, moving it was. They were on their way once more.

"Yes!" Darren shouted and punched the air.

"At last!" Maria Fernandez said as she climbed to her feet. She turned to Miss Grange. "I know we're not travelling very fast," she said, "but you would agree that we were *in motion*, no?"

"Certainly," said Miss Grange, looking at her, puzzled.

Maria Fernandez smiled and leant towards her conspiratorially. "I must powder my nose," she whispered.

Miss Grange laughed behind her hand. "Oh, I see," she said. "Yes, we're definitely moving! Thank Heavens!"

Vicky watched the Spanish woman strut down the aisle to the toilet opposite the stacked luggage area at the end of the carriage. With her fur coat, her crocodile-skin accessories and the gold that clattered softly as she walked, she looked an unlikely passenger in the buffet car of the train. Vicky wasn't the only one who thought so.

"Bet she's worth a few bob," said Simon Droy and winked at Darren. "Wonder if she's married."

"She is," Miss Grange informed him stiffly.

Behind her, Vicky heard Mandy Hurley drooling enviously. "I'd kill for a coat like that," she muttered.

Yeah, thought Vicky sourly. Lots of people kill for coats like that – and countless animals die in the process. She turned round and was about to say as much, but Darren placed his hand on her arm.

"Perhaps it's not the best time to get into a discussion about animal liberation," he said. The train continued along the track, slightly faster, but still terribly slow. "I've got a feeling this is going to be a long journey."

Vicky snorted, and looked round the carriage once more at the various characters she would have to spend it with. The vacuous couple at the buffet-bar. Smarmy wide-boy Droy. Starchy, disapproving Evelyn Grange. And the Patagonian Princess – dripping with gold and draped in dead animals. There wasn't one of them she'd choose to pass the time of day with.

Suddenly, the so-called British reserve that normally kept everyone to themselves seemed like the greatest invention ever, and inwardly, Vicky cursed the crash. Not because it had frightened her, nor because it had delayed the train – but because it had led to this sense of cameraderie amongst individuals who had absolutely nothing in common with one another.

She turned to Darren. "Why don't we go and find a seat somewhere else on the train," she suggested.

Before Darren could reply one way or the other, a voice piped up from behind him. "I'm afraid that won't be possible," it said.

Darren turned round. Vicky looked up. A man in a white shirt, bow-tie and waistcoat, who had appeared as if from nowhere, was standing in the aisle, smiling down at them sweetly. It was the buffet steward. He had black, slicked-back hair, a trim goatee beard and dark, darting eyes. A name-badge with *Nick* on it, was pinned to his lapel.

"You what?" said Darren.

"I said that it would not be possible for you to find alternative seating arrangements," Nick said, rubbing his hands together. Vicky shivered. Despite the constant smile on the steward's face as he spoke, there was a steely edge to his voice that she didn't like.

"But surely..." she began.

Nick's eyes glinted. "You are to remain here," he said, "until we reach our final destination. That is the procedure in a situation such as this." He smiled. "Your co-operation is much appreciated."

3

"Riff-raff," Maria Fernandez muttered to herself as she reached the toilet. She glanced back along the aisle of the carriage. Her upper lip curled with distaste.

The big short-haired man at the buffet was banging on the steel roller with renewed vigour, encouraged by the young blonde creature with the fake tan beside him. The man with the mobile was waving his arms about and chanting "*Scotland, Scotland*!" Then Miss Grange caught her eye and gave a little wave. Maria Fernandez pursed her lips.

Tedious creature! she thought. Augusto was right. I *should* have flown.

She looked away, turned the handle and pushed at the door, her bangles jangling.

And as for that scruffy couple sitting behind her! She'd noticed the way they glared at her fur coat and jewels – she'd seen it a thousand times before. The envious, hate-filled expressions on the faces of the little people who would, if they could only admit it to themselves, give anything to have what she had.

She stepped inside. The door slammed shut behind her.

Something was immediately wrong.

It was dark and cold and clammy inside the room. She fumbled around blindly for a light switch, but found none; her crocodile shoes paddled through a pool of water. An acrid stench filled her nostrils.

"Oh, but this is intolerable," she said, and turned to leave. She seized the door handle, turned and pulled.

Nothing happened.

"Typical!" she muttered.

When Augusto was in power, the trains in her own country had been spotlessly clean, perfectly maintained and always ran on time. Unlike this ... this...

She tugged the handle with more force. But the door was jammed. It would not open. A varnished fingernail broke off.

"Damn!" she exclaimed, and redoubled her efforts. "Open, blast you! *Open*!"

No matter how hard she struggled with the door, it refused to budge. Maria Fernandez wiped her forehead. Tears were beginning to well up in her eyes, blurring her vision and making her mascara run. She shuddered uncomfortably with cold, with fear.

"Help!" she cried out. "Help me. The door's stuck. *Help*!"

She paused and listened. No one came to her aid – yet she could hear something.

She cocked her head to one side, confused by the sounds beyond the room. The rattling of the steel roller and the football chanting had gone. Instead, the air outside was filled with desperate cries and pitiful moaning.

"Please, I beg you," howled a voice, louder than the rest. A girl's voice, fragile, frightened. "For the love of God, let me go, I implore you."

"Tell me! Tell me!" came the brutal reply, followed by a thud, a buzz and an agonized wail of pain which echoed through the air. "Tell me *everything*!"

Maria Fernandez shuddered. She wrapped her fur coat tightly around her and turned round. And as her eyes – accustomed to the gloom by now – scanned the filthy room, her heart began to thump with fear.

High up in the rough stone wall in front of her, was a small square window. Heavy iron bars were silhouetted against the moon outside. A wooden pallet stood below the window, with a greasy scrap of blanket crumpled up at one end. Beside the pallet, in the corner, was a bucket. It was from this that the choking smell was emanating.

The voice screamed, more terrible than ever. Starting with terror, Maria Fernandez found herself tottering across the wet, sticky floor. She tripped. She slipped. She fell heavily down on to all fours.

"No, no..." she whimpered. It couldn't be happening. "You're on a train," she told herself. "On your way to Scotland, where darling Augusto you will meet you in his sleek black car and whisk you off to the hunting lodge."

This prison cell – it wasn't real. It couldn't be. They had escaped. They had got away...

Suddenly, above the sound of human misery outside, she heard something else. A scratching. A squeaking. And a sleek, brown rat brushed past her fingers and scurried away.

"No!" she screeched, and leapt to her feet. Not rats. Anything but rats!

All round her, she could see their glinting eyes staring at her from the shadowy corners, while from every crack and crevice in the stone walls, more of the plump rodents squeezed through and plopped down on to the floor. They sniffed the air. They scratched; they squealed.

Hysteria rose from the pit of her stomach. Bile

burned her throat. She opened her mouth and screamed and screamed.

The rats were all round her now, scampering under her feet as she darted and dodged on her high heels, desperate to escape their inquisitive noses and quivering whiskers. She staggered forwards, hitched up her silk dress and climbed awkwardly on to the pallet. From the door opposite, she heard a steel plate sliding across to reveal a small rectangular hole. An eye appeared.

"Let me out of here!" she sobbed. "Please. Please. There's been a terrible mistake. Let me out!"

The eye blinked impassively. "There has been no mistake," said the voice.

The steel plate slammed shut.

"No! Stop!" Maria Fernandez cried out. She looked down at the floor, writhing with the squeaking, scratching vermin, and shuddered. Then back at the door. "Don't go!" she implored. "Please, don't go!"

Despite the rats, she knew she had to get to the door. To bring the guard back. To explain that it *was* a mistake after all. With her heart in her mouth she stared down giddily at the heaving mass of furry bodies. She counted to ten. She counted to ten again.

"Come on," she told herself. "You've got no choice. Go!"

Finally, she jumped down.

Her heel skewered one of the rats as she landed. It squealed piteously for a moment, then fell still. The other rats, driven to a frenzy by the sound of death and the smell of blood, leapt at it and began tearing away at its flesh.

Within a moment, there were rats all over her foot; nibbling round her ankle, scratching at her calf. Maria Fernandez moaned with terror and desperately kicked off her shoe – and the clinging rats. She retched emptily. Her mouth was parched. Her stomach gnawed with aching emptiness.

"Come back," she whispered breathlessly – and stumbled. She tottered forwards, fell against the door and...

A seering blue light jarred through her body.

Burnt hair. Blistered skin. Bulging eyeballs. And pain! Pain such as Maria Fernandez had never known before! Mind-numbing, gut-wrenching pain that coursed down every vein and seared every cell.

"*Everything*!" a voice screamed. "Tell us everything you know!"

Her eyes burned. Her ears screamed. And as convulsions racked her body – twisting her spine and slamming her teeth down on her tongue – she tumbled to the ground.

There she remained, a quivering, whimpering ball of misery and fear. Thirsty. Hungry. Cold.

The rats, emboldened by the stillness of the

creature in their midst, scurried closer. They poked and prodded. Their whiskers brushed against the warm skin.

Then, the bravest sunk its teeth into an exposed finger.

"No!" Maria Fernandez cried out. She flapped her hand about, but was too weak to shake it off. The rat clung on ferociously. It was joined by others. "Get off!" she whimpered. "Leave me alone."

She looked up at the door – still locked, and with the eye-hole shut – and was overwhelmed with a sense of utter despair.

"For the love of God, let me out of here," she whimpered.

But no one heard. No one came. She had been abandoned; left to die in this squalid cell.

"Please. I beg you." Her voice was little more than a sigh. "Please..."

4

As the train slowly gathered speed the buffet steward, Nick, continued through the carriage, filling a black bin-liner with the rubbish that had fallen to the ground. He dealt solicitously with the passengers who, now that someone official had finally turned up, were taking the opportunity to air their grievances.

"It was absolutely terrifying," Miss Grange was complaining. "And as for what actually happened, we're still none the wiser."

Nick smiled understandingly. "Everything will be explained in due course, madam," he said. "At the moment, however, the intercom system seems to be down. In fact," he said, as the lights flickered, "all the electrics seem to be a bit faulty. An announcement will be made the moment repairs have been effected."

"Yes, well," said Miss Grange, disarmed by his good-natured explanation. "I must know how long we've been delayed."

"Whatever the delay, we will be arriving at our destination at the time we were meant to arrive," Nick assured her. "It is a long journey. We'll make up the time we've lost later in the night."

"Not travelling at this speed," Simon Droy butted in. "We can't be going more than ten kilometres an hour."

"As I said, sir," said Nick, "we *will* be making up the time. Network Railways prides itself on its punctuality. And I personally—"

Suddenly, from the far end of the carriage, came the sound of furious banging. Nick spun round.

"What *do* you think you're doing?" he barked.

Greg Tolson and Mandy Hurley turned to look at him defiantly. Having abandoned the steel roller at the buffet, the pair of them were up at the front end of the carriage, between the toilet and the luggage racks, hammering on the connecting door. Nick strode towards them.

"The wilful damage of Network Railway property is a serious offence," he said.

"The bloody door to the next carriage is jammed," said Greg.

"It isn't jammed," said Nick. "It's locked."

Greg put his hands on his hips. "Then *unlock* it," he said.

"I'm afraid I can't do that, sir," said Nick.

"Why not?" Greg demanded. "Don't they trust you with a key."

Nick smiled. "I have a key," he said. "But not the necessary authorization to open it."

"But you could."

"The correct procedure must be followed," said Nick pleasantly.

"Which means?"

"I will unlock the door when I receive the relevant go-ahead. But not before."

"And how does that happen?"

"By intercom," said Nick.

"But the intercom's dead," Mandy butted in. "I just heard you telling him." She nodded towards Simon Droy, who was – like all the others – listening in with interest to the developing dispute.

"Precisely," said Nick patiently.

Greg stared down at the steward, lip curling. How he hated these jumped-up little officials. "You're telling me you can only open the door when you get the go-ahead over an intercom system that isn't working?" he said. The sound of Mandy's laughter beside him egged him on. "What are you?" he boomed. "Some kind of moron?"

"I would hope not, sir," said Nick. "Network Railways has a most stringent employment policy."

"Are you trying to be funny?" Greg demanded.

"Not at all, sir," said Nick.

The steward's unruffled response irritated Greg still further. He stooped down till his face – red and contorted with rage – was pressed into that of the smaller man. "Then see if you understand this," he said, his voice clipped and patronizing. "Before I came to the buffet car I put my jacket in the compartment where I have a seat. My wallet is in the jacket. I need it now." He glared menacingly. "So open the damned door!"

Vicky, who had been watching the whole incident unfold, turned to Darren.

"Bully," she muttered.

Darren shrugged. "He's got a point, though," he said. "Why *is* the door locked? Why shouldn't we leave the buffet car if we want to?"

"I don't know," said Vicky. "But the way he's talking to that poor bloke is inexcusable." And, as she watched Greg's thunderous face, she shuddered as memories of various people from the past flashed before her – Suzie Ingrams, Tasha Edmondson, Miss Prendergast her headmistress, Mr Peeves in the bank where she'd temped – people who had bullied *her*. Greg Tolson had the same aggressive body-language as her old tormentors; the same wicked glint of power and contempt in his eyes. He was clearly used to always getting his own way.

"Are you going to open that door, or not?" he roared.

"Not, sir," said Nick, and went to turn away.

Mandy looked at Greg and raised her eyebrows. "What a cheek!" she muttered.

Greg set his jaw. He was damned if he was going to be treated so dismissively by this officious, jumped-up little squit – particularly when he was trying to impress the athletic young Mandy. He stepped forwards, seized Nick by the front of his waistcoat and dragged him back round, and up towards his face.

"Don't you dare turn away from me when I'm speaking to you," he said.

Vicky couldn't see the buffet steward's face but, if he was like her, then she knew exactly what he must be feeling. Being intimidated like that left her jelly-like – numb, quivering and unable to react, either physically or verbally. It took her by surprise when she heard Nick speak.

"I would advise you to let me go at once, sir," he said calmly, coldly.

"Oh, would you?" said Greg. He turned, grinned at Mandy and lifted Nick further into the air, until his toes were barely scraping the floor. "And I suppose—"

There was a brief flash of red. Greg Tolson released Nick and flew back through the air. He thudded against the locked door, and slumped heavily to the floor. He did not move.

Mandy Hurley stepped forwards. She looked at Greg and then at Nick. "What have you done to him?" she said.

"Done?" said Nick. "He slipped." He leaned down and held out his hand to help Greg back to his feet.

Greg turned away. "I can get myself up," he said gruffly. It was bad enough being floored in front of the gorgeous Mandy Hurley, without being helped back to his feet by his attacker.

What *had* he done? Greg wondered. The way the steward's eyes had seemed to glow red; the sudden shock that had abruptly passed from his body into his own... Had the weedy little man mastered some weird kind of self-defence? Some inscrutable martial art? He struggled to his feet with as much dignity as he could muster.

"Nothing broken I trust, sir," Nick said.

Greg muttered under his breath.

"Excellent!" came the reply. "And I am pleased to tell you that you will not be needing your wallet. The complimentary buffet voucher I saw you with earlier allows you to have any refreshments of your choice throughout the journey."

"Yeah, I've got one too," said Mandy hotly. "But the buffet's shut."

Nick turned and looked at the closed shutters as if seeing them for the first time. "So it is," he said. "It will open presently."

"When?" Mandy said sharply.

Nick looked at her and smiled sweetly. "When I am ready," he said, nodding at the bag of rubbish. "When I have finished clearing up. And I have to check you all off against my official list of voucher holders, of course. But that shouldn't take long. As soon as I am able, I'll open up." His eyes twinkled. "All right?"

Mandy opened and closed her mouth a couple of times, unsure whether to speak her mind or not. Greg hadn't slipped, she knew that. Something strange had happened to him: something she didn't want happening to her.

"I'm very hungry," she said simply.

"I'm sure you are," said Nick. "That pumped-up body of yours must burn up the calories like nobody's business."

And with that he turned away, picked up the bin-liner and walked off, leaving Mandy opening and shutting her mouth again like a goldfish.

"But what do you actually *do*?" Darren interrupted.

He and Simon Droy had been talking – or rather, Simon had been talking while Darren had been listening in silence – for the last fifteen minutes. His question was the first time he'd managed to get a word in edgeways.

"Do?" said Simon. He ran his fingers through his hair and chuckled thoughtfully. "I'm Mr Fixit, aren't I? I wheel and deal. Bit of this, bit of that. You name it, I can get hold of it." He winked. "And at *very* competitive prices."

Vicky scowled as she continued to stare resolutely out through the window, though there was nothing to see. "You mean, it's nicked," she said.

Simon Droy winced as though someone had just scraped their fingernails down a blackboard.

"Slander, I call that," he said. "*Nicked*! I mean, do I look like the kind of bloke who'd deal in stolen goods?"

Vicky snorted, but said nothing.

"So, what kind of thing might you be interested in?" he said, turning his attention back to Darren. "Computer hardware? Software? CD player? Camcorder?"

Darren smiled and rubbed his index finger and thumb together ruefully.

"Money?" said Simon. "You don't want to worry about that. The things I've got are so cheap I'm practically giving them away."

Vicky turned round and glared at him. "We're not interested," she said. "OK?"

Simon Droy held his hands up defensively. "All right, all right," he said. "Don't get your knickers in a twist. I was just trying to be friendly. You won't get very far in this world if you're not friendly..." He pulled a handkerchief from his pocket and mopped his glistening brow. "My God, it's getting hot in here," he said. He removed his jacket, loosened his tie and undid the top button of his shirt. "Isn't anyone else hot?"

Behind them, Miss Grange, who was fanning herself with her copy of *The Lady* magazine, agreed. "And the trouble is," she added, "the hotter it becomes, the less agreeable the air."

She opened her handbag and pulled out a slim bottle of scent which she smeared on her wrists, rubbed behind her ears, and sprayed in the air around her. There were mutters of complaint from some of the others but, studiously ignoring them, Miss Grange gave a final blast of the perfume for good luck, and returned the bottle to her bag.

At that moment, Nick passed with his bin-liner. He returned a holdall to the luggage rack and hung Simon's jacket on one of the hooks provided. He sniffed. He winced.

"Dear, dear," he said. "Is that the toilet I can smell?"

He walked on, leaving Darren, Vicky and Simon in fits of laughter, and Miss Grange open-mouthed with indignation.

"It ... it's *Chanel*!" she spluttered.

Nick turned and smiled broadly. "I don't think so," he said. "I'd better check."

"But it's engaged," said Miss Grange.

"Engaged?" said Nick. He looked around the carriage. "Ah yes," he said. "The charming Latin

American lady." A look of concern passed over his amiable features. He sniffed and winced a second time. "I do hope she's all right."

"Course, if you *are* short of money..." Simon was saying to Darren.

Vicky raised her eyebrows and turned back to the window. She shivered with apprehension. The blackness outside was still impenetrable. Surely they couldn't be in the same tunnel – yet if they weren't, then why were there no streetlamps or headlights to be seen?

She wiped the condensation away and pressed her face against the glass.

There was nothing there. Nothing at all, save the persistent, uneasy feeling she had that they were being watched.

"It's lucrative. It's foolproof. And it's as legal as it needs to be," Simon Droy explained.

"What is?" asked Darren.

Simon winked conspiratorially. "Insurance," he said. "Pay a pittance of a premium and claim the earth. It's like buying a lottery ticket – with one major difference. You can't lose!"

"But, what kind of premium?" said Darren, interested despite himself.

Vicky sighed and closed her eyes. It would be nice not to have to count the pennies – after all, if the tenner hadn't been such a big deal, they could be sitting in their own plush seats rather than being locked up in the buffet car with a load of unpleasant strangers. And what an appalling bunch they were!

A wide-boy. A bully. The vain, the stuck-up and the unspeakable! And, with the door to the adjoining carriage locked, no way of escaping any of them.

Darren was right. It was going to be a very, very long journey indeed.

5

Nick stopped by the locked toilet door, cocked his head to one side and listened. He raised his hand and tapped discreetly.

"Hello?" he said.

There was no reply.

"Hello-o!" He tried the door handle. "Hello?"

Miss Grange, who had been monitoring the situation closely, got up from her seat and walked down the aisle to Nick.

"Is there a problem?" she said. "She's been in there ages. I'm a qualified nurse," she added. "Retired now, of course, but with over forty years' experience there isn't much I haven't seen."

Nick appraised her thoughtfully. "I daresay there

isn't," he said. He turned and knocked on the door, louder this time.

From inside the cubicle came the sound of soft moaning. Nick and Miss Grange exchanged glances.

"I don't like the sound of that," said Miss Grange. She pushed past him and banged on the door herself. "Miss Fernandez," she said. "Can you hear me? What's wrong?" She turned to Nick. "You must open the door. At once."

"That was precisely what I was about to do, madam," he said. "If you would step aside."

He removed a coin from his pocket, inserted it into the screw above the *Engaged* sign and turned. They both heard the inside bolt slide across. Miss Grange seized the handle and pushed.

As the door opened, she was struck by a blast of cold, damp, foul-smelling air. Voices clamoured and wailed. Boots pounded. Dogs barked. But just for an instant.

Then it was gone.

Miss Grange turned to Nick, eyes wide with horror. "Wh... What was that?" she said.

"What was *what*?" he said amiably as he pushed the door right open. The pair of them looked in.

Maria Fernandez was slumped in the corner of the cubicle, shaking uncontrollably. The expression on her drawn, puffy face was one of utter terror. Her brow was furrowed, her skin was the colour of wax; her eyes stared back at them, unblinking.

For a second time, Miss Grange pushed past Nick. She splashed through the water on the floor, crouched down and pressed her hand against the woman's clammy brow.

Maria Fernandez shrieked. "Leave me alone!" And she began slapping the air all round her hysterically. Miss Grange fell backwards as a hand struck her face. Maria Fernandez began sobbing. "Just let me be!" she wailed.

"She's delusional," Miss Grange gasped as, nursing her scratched cheek, she withdrew.

"Possibly," said Nick. "Possibly not." He stepped forwards and spoke calmly to the panic-stricken woman. "There, there," he said. "You're all right now."

A flicker of recognition passed across Maria Fernandez's features.

"It *is* the toilet," she muttered, and looked up. "I … the light must have gone."

Nick looked up and inspected the bulb. "It seems to be fine now," he said. He reached down to help her to her feet. "These things can be very traumatic," he said sympathetically. "I do understand."

Maria Fernandez nodded, but said nothing. How *could* he understand? She didn't understand herself. Yet she knew well enough what she had just experienced. She knew, too, that she shouldn't reveal it to anyone – not even darling Augusto. *Especially* not Augusto. He would take it as a sign of guilt: a sign of weakness.

"So, what happened?" Greg Tolson asked Miss Grange when she returned. He and Mandy Hurley had sat down near the others.

"A funny turn, that's all," said Miss Grange sharply. "It happens to the best of us."

"And she certainly thinks she's better than most, by the look of her," Simon Droy commented.

At that moment, Maria Fernandez herself appeared at the door, supported on Nick's arm. All eyes turned towards her.

"I'm quite capable of reaching my seat by myself," she said, shaking him off.

"Of course you are, madam," said Nick.

As the train continued to jolt slowly along the tracks, Maria Fernandez made her way giddily up the central aisle. She kept her head held high, ignoring the stares of the others in the carriage.

"She looks as if she's seen a ghost," said Mandy.

"*Whoooerr*!" went Greg. "The haunted toilet!" And he and Simon sniggered to themselves.

"Oh, don't be so mean!" Mandy protested.

But Greg was getting into his stride now. "The ghost of Ebenezer Grimshaw," he continued, his voice low and doom-laden. "Flushed away all those years ago, never to be seen again." He turned to Mandy and opened his eyes wide. "Until now!"

She laughed. Darren was laughing, too. Even Vicky couldn't help smiling. The situation was too ridiculous! The woman had entered the toilet, arrogant and self-possessed – and come out a nervous wreck. Whatever had happened inside looked far more serious than "a funny turn".

"Are you all right, my dear?" said Miss Grange, fussing round her with a cup of water.

"Would you like a boiled sweet?" said Mandy, pulling a bag from her small rucksack.

Maria Fernandez's lips tightened with irritation. "I don't want anything, thank you," she said. "I'm quite all right. Just a little chilled." She wrapped herself in her fur coat, and stared down at the table.

The others looked at one another in surprise.

"Chilled?" Mandy mouthed to Greg. Having already rid herself of her fleece and leggings, she was down to a pair of lycra cycle shorts and a singlet.

Greg shrugged.

"But it must be thirty degrees in here," she said.

"At least!" said Darren, taking it as a cue to strip off down to his T-shirt.

Greg Tolson looked around for the buffet steward. He was heading back up the carriage, carrying a bucket and mop. "Here, Nick," he said. "I thought you were going to open that buffet."

Nick turned and smiled back at him. "Sir?" he said.

For a moment, Greg shivered. Those eyes were on him again, piercing and intense. Despite the close proximity of the others, he felt his confidence draining away from him. Not that he was about to lose face...

"It's hot," he said. "We're all thirsty."

"Of course you are, sir. But as you can see," he said, raising the bucket and mop. "I'm a bit tied up at the moment. As soon as I've cleaned up the toilet, I'll be right with you." And, offering no chance for Greg to respond, he turned away and continued up the aisle.

Greg's face burned red and his fists clenched. He wasn't used to being dealt with so dismissively. Given what had happened earlier, however, he was wary about pushing the matter too far with the steward. Yet his anger would not go away. He turned round and glared at Maria Fernandez.

"So what *were* you doing in the toilet?" he said.

Miss Grange answered for her. "She fainted," she said.

"And wet the floor in the process," Greg snorted.

Mandy and Simon sniggered. Vicky tutted. The man really was a bully, and she found herself agreeing with Miss Grange when she told him not to be so insensitive.

"Insensitive?" sneered Greg. "I'm dying of thirst

here and our buffet steward can do nothing about it because he's mopping up the mess in the toilet."

Miss Grange turned away. "Ignore him, dear," she said to Maria Fernandez, and patted her hand.

Maria Fernandez looked up and stared ahead. It was clear from the blankness of her expression that she hadn't heard a single word that had been said.

She had been back in the prison cell, dragged back there by her memories, which were triggering other memories of their own. She remembered the words which had echoed down the dark corridors. *For the love of God, let me go, I implore you!* they had cried out. Desperate words. Familiar words. She thought of the smuggled note she had received from Rosa.

It had ended with those very same words.

At the time, she had screwed up the paper and tossed it into the bin. She didn't want to know about the conditions in the cold, dark cell; of the rats, of the torture... Yet now, she couldn't get it out of her head.

Rosa Vicario had been her personal maid. She was a nineteen-year-old, already with two daughters to look after and – since her husband, Juan, was a known supporter of the opposition who had been apprehended in the first wave of arrests – a single mother. In a fit of sympathetic madness, Maria had employed her, and Rosa had taken up her post in the Presidential Palace in August. By December, she was in prison, accused – by Maria Fernandez herself – of spying for the rebels...

But she *was* a spy, Maria Fernandez told herself as she wrestled with her conscience. She was passing on key information to her brother, Luis, a notorious terrorist. It was my duty to inform the authorities: to protect my country, my government – my dear husband...

Yes, protecting Augusto. That was the true reason for what she had done. She knew that Rosa had been sleeping with him and feared it might lead to blackmail.

A little siren, she was – no better than a common prostitute. Always making eyes at dear Augusto. Trying to seduce him under her very nose. She was dangerous. Treacherous. Maria Fernandez had had no choice but to make her leave; to make her disappear – for ever.

"Lock her up and throw away the key," she'd commanded.

Now though, she knew what the girl had been through. She had tasted her sense of injustice, her terror, her despair. She had felt the pain of that searing blue light. The blistered skin. The swollen tongue. The pain that had burned into every single cell of her body. And that moment of hopelessness in the cold, damp cell when she realized that the guard was never coming back; that she would die there, and the loathsome rats would devour her dead body.

But how? What terrible force – without or within – had brought her to this knowledge?

She felt a warm, comforting hand on her own and looked up nervily. The foolish retired nurse was speaking.

"Losing consciousness can be a shock to the system," she said softly. "It's disorientating. It's..."

Maria Fernandez turned towards her. There was horror in her eyes. "Do you believe in evil?" she said, her voice little more than a whisper.

Miss Grange's jaw dropped. "Evil?" she said. The nape of her neck tingled unpleasantly. "It isn't something I've ever given much thought to."

Maria Fernandez frowned. "And I don't mean simply the absence of good," she said. "But something ... some malevolent force that ... that..." She shivered, and mopped her glistening, waxen forehead. Although she had resolved to remain silent about what she had experienced, her desire to make sense of it all proved stronger. "There was something in there," she said. "I felt it." As she fixed the other woman with her penetrating gaze, something came back to her. "And so did you," she said.

Miss Grange glanced round uneasily. She didn't want the other passengers to hear what they were talking about. Flushed with the arrogance of youth, they would only ridicule them.

"Felt what?" she said cautiously.

"When the door opened," said Maria Fernandez, "I... I saw you flinch."

"Flinch?" she repeated. "It was the shock of seeing you on the floor."

Maria Fernandez's eyes narrowed. "Are you sure that was the only reason?" she said.

Miss Grange nodded, but even as she did so, the moment when Nick unlocked the door and she had pushed it ajar came back to her. The blast of cold, damp, foul-smelling air; the shouting, and wailing.

"Well?" said Maria Fernandez.

"I think the window must have been open," Miss Grange replied. "It *was* a bit chilly – and there was a wind howling."

Maria Fernandez sniffed and patted at her eyes with her handkerchief. "The window wasn't the opening kind," she said.

"Then there must be some other perfectly rational explanation," said Miss Grange. "And in answer to your first question, no, I don't believe in evil. Spirits, ghouls, things that go bump in the night – so far as I'm concerned the vast majority of them are conjured up by a bad conscience..." She winced, realizing what she had said.

"Bad conscience," Maria Fernandez repeated flatly.

"Oh, not that I'm implying that you... I mean, far be it from me to ... to..." She smiled awkwardly. "You fainted. You took a fall. It is common in such cases for the person to … to imagine things." She leant forward in her seat until their faces were almost touching. "But tell me, what *did* you see in there?"

Maria Fernandez pulled away, unsure whether it was concern or morbid curiosity motivating the other woman's interest. She certainly looked like the gossipy type.

"I… I can't remember," she said.

"Come now," Miss Grange said softly. "A problem shared is a problem halved, that's what I always say."

"All the same," said Maria Fernandez curtly. She pulled her hand away from Miss Grange's tight grip and sat back in her chair. "But thank you for your sympathy. I shall consult my doctor at the earliest opportunity…"

Miss Grange smiled. For all her airs and graces, she knew that Maria Fernandez was lying. Can't remember, she thought. Oh, you can remember all right. Some horrid little secret, no doubt. But I shall get it out of you yet. I always do.

Behind them, Greg was holding court in an attempt to regain his dignity after being first floored and then snubbed by Nick.

"A couple of pelts short of a fur coat," he was saying under his breath, and screwed his finger into his right temple.

Mandy giggled. Simon and Darren chuckled.

"Course, that's all we need," Greg continued. "Being locked inside a carriage with a nutter."

Vicky turned on him. "You heard what that Miss Grange said," she hissed. "She passed out."

"Yeah, right!" said Greg. His voice dropped to a whisper again. "Then how come they've been talking about ghosts and ghoulies then?"

They all glanced round at Maria Fernandez, who caught their eye and turned away haughtily.

"They weren't," said Vicky, shocked.

"They were," said Greg. "I heard them."

"Maybe she had, like, some sort of religious experience," said Mandy. "You know, like St Paul on the road to Damascus and that."

"What, in a bog on the Scotland Express?" said Greg. "Do me a favour! I'm telling you, we're travelling with a fruit cake."

Vicky turned away. The unseen presence seemed to glower back at her from beyond the window. Why could she still see nothing out there? she wondered uneasily.

Once, years ago when she was six or seven, she and her parents had spent a weekend in a country manor-house: Irton Grange, it was called. That first evening, the owner – a gaunt, stooped man with a squint – had regaled them with tales of the Irton ghost over dinner.

"She walks at midnight," he'd said. "The white

lady. And woe betide any with blood on their hands..."

At bedtime, she lay under the heavy covers, her whole body shaking with foreboding as the midnight hour had ticked closer and closer. Finally, unable to stand it any more, she had slipped from her bed, left the room and crept down the stairs to the front door. Neither her mum nor her dad ever discovered that she spent both nights at Irton Grange sleeping on the back seat of the car.

Now, with all the talk of spirits and evil, Vicky was gripped by the same icy shivers of apprehension. This time, however, the brooding atmosphere outside offered no sanctuary. Even if it had been possible to reach it – which, with the carriage sealed and the train now travelling too fast for her to get off, it wasn't – she had the disturbing feeling that leaving the buffet car would be like jumping out of the frying pan and into the fire.

"Darren," she whispered, and took hold of his arm.

He turned and looked at her, his face smiling at something Simon Droy had just said. "What is it?" he asked.

"Darren, I'm frightened," she said.

Darren frowned. "Frightened?" he said. "What of?"

Vicky shrugged. What could she say? That she thought the carriage was haunted; that the darkness outside was filling her with unnamed terror? It made no sense. Perhaps Greg Tolson was right: perhaps they were travelling with a nutter after all – but it wasn't Maria Fernandez. "Just, I dunno ... frightened of what's going to happen," she said vaguely.

Darren hugged her warmly. "Come on, Vicks," he said. "Chin up."

Vicky pulled away and looked at Darren, all tearful and smiley. "I'm being stupid," she said. "Just ignore me. It's just – I don't know. First me. Now her. She looked so shaken up. I don't understand..."

"There's nothing *to* understand," said Darren. "You heard what they said. She fainted." He shrugged. "The shock of the crash must have upset her more than she realized."

Vicky nodded. "You're probably right," she said.

"I know I'm right," said Darren. "Trust me."

"All right, then," said Vicky with a smile. "Mind if I use your jacket?"

Darren shook his head. Vicky took the padded bomber jacket, folded it into a square and propped it up between the backrest of the chair and the window. She leant her head back.

"I'm going to try and get some sleep," she said.

"You do that," said Darren.

Vicky smiled and closed her eyes.

At first, as the lulling conversation continued

around her, she felt better. The train, still gathering pace, juddered rhythmically. *Clunkety-clunk, clunkety-clunk*. Her body felt heavy with sleep, yet her mind was alert.

There *was* something out there in the darkness. She was sure of it. With her ear so close to the window, she could hear it – or them – howling, screaming, wailing...

Her eyes snapped open. The distant cries faded abruptly. She sat up and looked around, more bewildered than ever.

"Had a good nap?" said Darren.

"A nap?" said Vicky. "I've only just shut my eyes."

Darren laughed. "You've been snoring for a good hour," he said. "Hasn't she?" he added, turning to the others.

"Certainly has," said Simon. Mandy nodded. Greg sat back, let his mouth drop open and snored and whistled loudly.

"Witnesses!" said Darren.

"But ... I can't have," she said. She nodded up to the far end of the carriage where the steel roller was still down. "Why isn't the buffet open yet?"

"Yeah, good question," said Greg, looking round irritably for Nick.

"But you definitely were asleep," said Darren.

Vicky nodded. If she *had* been asleep, at least that would explain the curious voices – she'd simply been dreaming. So why did that thought not make her feel better? Why was it more alarming to know that the distant wailing might all have been in her imagination?

She leaned forwards in her seat and pulled the sweat-soaked T-shirt away from her back. It was so hot in the carriage; so stiflingly hot. She could barely breathe. She felt hemmed in, giddy. All round her, the whole carriage seemed to be swaying – zooming in and telescoping away – as it clattered on through the empty, black landscape outside.

What if we're the only ones, she found herself wondering for the second time, and her heart beat so fast her temples pounded. What if the whole world has disappeared, and we're the only ones left?

It was a thought she'd had so many times before: on the empty streets on her way to do her early-morning paper-round, on an almost deserted underground station, in a lift, on a bus, on a plane... Usually it was just a game she played, imagining the scenario that had led to her and her few companions being cut off from the rest of the population.

But this was different. Utterly different. Never before had she been so totally overwhelmed with the dread that gripped her now...

Just then, the electronic trill of a mobile phone

cut through the air and Mandy, Greg, Simon and Maria Fernandez all began rummaging through their pockets and bags.

Vicky sighed with childlike relief. Of course they weren't on their own. Of course the world had not come to an end. Someone – someone from out there – was trying to make contact.

"It's not mine," Greg announced, shaking his mobile. "Can't even get a signal."

"Nor mine," said Mandy.

Without saying a word, Maria Fernandez returned her own phone to her crocodile handbag.

The insistent ringing continued.

"It must be mine, then," said Simon Droy. He stood up and frisked his trouser pockets. "I can't..." he frowned. Then he noticed his jacket hanging on the hook where Nick had put it. "Don't stop," he muttered as he rooted through the pockets. "Don't... Ah, here it is."

He pulled the phone out, pressed the answer button and put it to his ear. "Hello?" he said.

The others watched with idle interest as he clamped his hand over his other ear and frowned with concentration.

"Hello?" he said again. He turned away, and walked down the aisle towards the back of the train. "Hello? You'll have to speak up, I... Oh, hello. Yes, speaking."

Greg craned his neck and looked up and down

the carriage. "Where is Nick anyway?" he said. "He finished mopping up in the toilet ages ago."

"He said something about a list," Mandy reminded him. "That he had to tick us off before we could use our vouchers."

Darren nodded towards the door marked *Private* which led into the buffet-bar behind the steel roller. "I think I saw him go back in there," he said. "And anyway," he added, turning to Vicky, "what are these vouchers? Why haven't *we* got any?"

Vicky shrugged.

"I got mine when I bought my ticket," said Mandy.

Greg nodded. "Me too," he said. He glanced over at the closed buffet. "I might have known there'd be a hitch."

"You know what they say," said Mandy. "There's no such thing as a free lunch."

"Certainly not on this train," said Greg irritably. "Thanks to that smarmy little steward..." The train lurched abruptly into a tight bend, sending him staggering across the aisle. He clutched hold of an overhead rail and looked round, a sheepish grin on his face. "Still, at least we're picking up a bit of speed," he said.

The others nodded and fell silent. From the far end of the carriage came the mumble of Simon's increasingly animated conversation. Miss Grange was opening her second flask of tea. Maria

Fernandez was inspecting her nails. Vicky peered out into the blackness outside. "Where do you think we are?"

Darren shrugged. "Impossible to tell," he said. "Did anyone notice the last station we passed through."

Mandy and Greg shook their heads.

"I haven't seen *any* stations," said Vicky. "Not a single one." Her voice dropped to a low whisper. "Something just doesn't seem right..."

At that moment, Simon cried out. The others spun round to see him flapping his arms about, his face twisted with horror.

"No!" he was shouting. "NO!"

6

Simon hadn't recognized the voice at the other end of the line. It was high-pitched, sibilant and seemed to be struggling not to burst out laughing.

It was a bit like receiving one of the phone calls *he* used to make when he was a boy, to people he'd find in the telephone directory with names like Smelly or Shufflebottom. "Are you Smelly?" he'd ask. "Well why don't you have a bath, then?" *Snigger snigger*. "Is that a Shufflebottom I can hear?" *Snigger snigger*. But why would anyone bother phoning him: there was nothing funny about the name Simon Droy...

"Who is that?" he demanded.

"You don't know who I am?" came the reply.

"If I knew, I wouldn't have asked," said Simon impatiently.

The person could control his amusement no longer and Simon had to hold the phone away as the sound of loud, cackling laughter bellowed from the earpiece. "I am your worst nightmare!" the voice screamed.

Simon stabbed at the off button furiously. The voice continued.

"And you won't silence me that easily," it taunted.

Simon glanced round him nervously. Why wouldn't the mobile allow itself to be switched off? Who *was* at the other end?

"Wh... What do you want?" he asked.

"I am the messenger!" the voice screeched triumphantly. "Turn round and receive the glad tidings."

"Turn round?" Simon muttered. "But I..."

"Turn round!" the voice barked.

It was behind him now, loud and echoing. Bewildered, fearful, Simon Droy did as he was told: he turned slowly round and stared ahead of him. He frowned, unable to make any sense of what lay before him. Instead of being in the railway buffet car he seemed to be standing in a dark and cavernous warehouse.

"What's going on?" he muttered nervously.

"Patience," hissed the voice – not from the mobile, but from the swirling shadows themselves.

Simon peered into the darkness. His legs were shaking. His mouth was dry. He looked down at his trembling hands and saw, to his horror, that the mobile phone had disappeared. In its place was a torch.

The voice cackled unpleasantly. "Over here!" it jeered. "Over here."

Switching on the torch, Simon shone the bright cone of light into the depths of the warehouse.

"Not there. *Here*!" came the voice, followed by more laughter.

Simon swung the beam of light around.

"No, *here*!" taunted the voice from behind him now.

"Where?" said Simon increasingly desperate. "Where?"

No matter where he shone the light, he could see nothing but the light itself as it bounced back off the thickening air. Misty it was, foggy – becoming denser and denser. Suddenly, he heard the sound of crackling, and he knew with instant and absolute certainty that it wasn't fog at all. It was smoke – thick, black smoke. Chemical. Pungent.

"And you know what they say," the voice continued, screeching with malicious glee. "There's no smoke without *fire*!"

As the word echoed round the warehouse, there

came an almighty WHOOPF! and the air itself seemed to burst into flames.

"No, no, no..." Simon whimpered. "NO!"

"What in God's name's the matter with Simon?" said Mandy.

The others all turned and stared. He was spinning round, arms flapping at something only he could see. He coughed. He choked. Tears streamed down over his bright red cheeks as he ran first this way, then that way, before stopping abruptly, shielding his face, and backing away.

Greg started laughing. He nodded back to Maria Fernandez. "Taking the piss, isn't he?" he said.

"No! No!" Simon screeched all the louder. "There's got to be a way out. There's just got to be."

Vicky trembled and grasped hold of Darren's arm. "I... I don't like it," she whispered.

"OK, Simon," Greg shouted down the carriage. "Joke over, mate. Come and sit down."

But Simon gave no sign that he had heard or even seen him. Flailing wildly now, he was banging and clattering about in a panicked frenzy; knocking into the walls, the windows, the door at the back of the carriage.

"Stop it!" he screamed. "*Help*! HELP!"

"He means it," said Vicky, alarmed. "He needs help."

Greg snorted. "After you," he said.

"Typical," Vicky muttered as she pushed past Darren and started up the aisle.

"What's the matter with him?" Mandy asked.

"Search me," said Greg. "Having a fit? Losing his marbles?"

"Whatever it is," Maria Fernandez commented, "you can be sure that it is more real to him than reality itself."

Vicky froze.

"What do you mean?" said Mandy.

"He is experiencing something malevolent," she said darkly. "As to what it is, we can only guess, for only he knows what he can see and hear and feel..." She shuddered. "And why."

Mandy stepped forwards. "What did *you* experience?" she asked.

Maria Fernandez stiffened. "That is no concern of yours," she said. A humourless smile flickered across her face. "Or perhaps it is simply that there are two 'nutters' in the carriage."

"Hear, hear!" said Greg.

"But we can't just leave him like that," said Miss Grange as, stumbling around blindly, Simon continued to knock himself about.

Greg snorted. "Just watch me," he said.

Vicky turned away impatiently, and walked back along the aisle. The look on Simon Droy's face as he spun round left her breathless with anxiety.

Never before had she witnessed such pain, such terror, such distress. Eyes rolling and hair on end, the man – previously so smug – was a gibbering wreck.

"Help me!" he screamed. "Put it out. Put it out *now*!"

"Put what out?" said Vicky. She stepped forwards. As she did so, Simon swung round. His open hand smacked into the side of her jaw sending her spinning round and crashing to the floor.

"Vicky!" shouted Darren, leaping to his feet.

The fire was all round him now, with the flames lapping at his clothes, licking at his skin. And the heat! Like the blast from a furnace, it scalded his eyeballs and scorched his lungs. He could barely breathe and the little air there was was thick with the stench of burning hair, skin, nails, flesh. He looked down, and gasped with horror.

It was *his* hair burning, *his* skin crumpling and nails curling, *his* flesh hissing in the searing heat. He was being burned alive!

"Hel meh…" his voice rasped, barely human now, as he collapsed to the ground and curled himself up into a tight ball. "Hel…"

But it was no use. No help was on its way. He would never manage to escape the inferno which had engulfed him. The flames burned more intensely, setting his clothes on fire, his shoes, his body.

I didn't mean to, he thought desperately as his tears vaporized and were gone. It wasn't supposed to be like that. It really wasn't...

7

"I'm sure it wasn't," came a soothing voice. "It was just one of those things."

Simon flinched. It was almost as though the words were coming from inside his head. He uncurled, opened his eyes – and cried out for joy.

He was still in the buffet car, still heading north – still alive. With a sudden jerk of panic, he brought his hands round for inspection. They were as they should be: skin, smooth; nails, straight. He reached up and felt for his hair. It was still there...

"Thank God!" he moaned.

Nick laughed affably. "Come on, now, sir," he said. "Let's get you up off the floor and back to your seat." He nodded towards the mobile phone lying beside him. "Bad news it must have been to make you collapse like that. My commiserations."

Simon said nothing as he let himself be helped to his feet. He looked round the carriage. Everything was back where it should be – the seats, the aisle, the closed buffet-bar – just as before. Yet the memory of the conflagration persisted. With the temperature in the carriage now hotter than ever, he couldn't help imagining that, at any moment, the whole place was about to burst into flames once again.

"You're all right now, sir," said Nick reassuringly as he shepherded him down the aisle and into his seat. "You just take it easy for a moment."

Simon looked up and nodded his thanks. As he glanced round, he saw six pairs of eyes staring at him with a mixture of helplessness and hostility. Unable to meet their gaze, he placed his arms on the table in front of him and lay his head down.

He kept his eyes open, despite the weariness which had overcome him. Even in the time it took to blink, his vision filled with the terrible blaze. Simon knew that if he closed them completely – worse still, if he drifted off to sleep – the fire would return. And next time he might not be so lucky.

He chuckled grimly. *Lucky*? Could he seriously call himself *lucky*?

*　　*　　*

The atmosphere among the other passengers had changed. With Simon Droy sitting in their midst – head down, staring blindly at the window and occasionally giggling to himself – none of them wanted to speak about what might have happened to him. Yet no one could think of anything else. And so, tongue-tied, they simply stared – until Simon himself spoke up.

"I know you're all looking at me," he said weakly. "Please don't."

One by one, the others realized he could see them reflected in the window, and looked away, embarrassed. Miss Grange asked Maria Fernandez whether she would care for some more tea. Greg attempted to engage Mandy in a little more light-hearted banter. But every conversation was doomed before it began.

Darren looked up to see Nick hurrying back along the corridor to the door marked *Private*. "Are you going to open the buffet, or what?" he called out impatiently.

Nick turned and smiled broadly. "All in due course, sir," he said. "All in due course. I am duty bound to follow the correct procedure." And with that, he disappeared inside once again – behind the closed buffet-bar.

Darren looked at Vicky. "What *is* happening?" he said.

"I don't know," said Vicky. She shook her head.

"But I keep having the horrible feeling that that Nick character is concealing something from us. Refusing to unlock the door to the rest of the train, keeping the buffet closed..."

"And the way he dealt with Maria Fernandez and Simon," Darren said in a hushed whisper. "He didn't seem at all concerned by the way they were acting."

"Or surprised," Vicky whispered back. "It was almost as though he knew what Simon was going through..."

The pair of them fell silent and turned, as one, to look at Maria Fernandez.

"Do you think *she* knows what's going on?" Darren hissed.

Vicky shrugged. "Why don't you ask her?"

Darren grinned sheepishly. "Why don't *you*?" he said. "She's far more likely to talk to you."

Vicky knew he was probably right. With his heavy boots and confrontational haircut Maria Fernandez would most likely be alarmed if he went up to speak to her – particularly since his T-shirt with its black lettering was an incitement to "*Screw the rich*!" Vicky knew, of course that, while not exactly a pose, the anarchist clothes and haircut had more to do with practicality than politics. Inside, Darren was a marshmallow!

"OK," she said. "I'll see what I can find out."

As Vicky squeezed out past Darren, Miss

Grange was also on the move. She left her seat, headed up the aisle to the rack of luggage and began rummaging through a large holdall on wheels. Vicky crossed to where Maria Fernandez was sitting, alone now beside her folded fur coat. She cleared her throat.

The woman looked up. She was older than Vicky had thought. Deep lines were etched across her forehead, while the puffy flesh around her jowls and neck sagged. "Can I help you?" she said, her voice husky, imperious.

"Do you mind if I sit down?" said Vicky politely. She wiped her palm on the seat of her jeans without thinking, and held out her hand. "My name's Vicky Amis," she said.

"Maria Fernandez," the woman replied, as she brushed her fingers airily past Vicky's outstretched palm.

Vicky sat down. Behind her, she could hear Greg and Mandy giggling. At first she thought that they were laughing at her for going over to speak to Maria Fernandez, and she glanced round to silence them with one of her glares. But they hadn't even noticed her. Sitting closely together and stripped to the minimum acceptable for a public place, they had eyes only for each other.

"You've got the most amazing body I've ever seen," Greg was mumbling.

Mandy ran her hands over Greg's shoulders.

"You're not so bad yourself," she said. "You must work out," she purred.

"So must you," said Greg, pulling her towards him.

Vicky turned back, and had to suppress a smile as she saw the expression of distaste etched across Maria Fernandez's face. "In my country, such behaviour would not be tolerated," she snapped.

"And which country is that?" said Vicky, leaping at the chance of a way in to conversation.

Maria smiled dreamily as she told her. "The most beautiful country in the world," she said, "with white sandy beaches, snow-capped mountains, virgin rainforest... Paradise." Her eyes hardened. "Yet how ungrateful are its people. They rioted, they rampaged, they ran amok – and despite everything that Augusto did for them..."

Augusto Fernandez! The name set bells ringing in Vicky's head. Elena, from the basement of the squat, had told her all about him.

Her three brothers, Julio, Raoul and Gabriel, counted among the many *missing ones* who'd vanished under his brutal regime. Elena herself had had to flee for her life from this so-called paradise. The previous year, she had persuaded Vicky and Darren to accompany her on a huge demonstration calling for his overthrow. Three months later, that had happened. Now, she seemed to be face to face with the wife of the ex-dictator.

How have the mighty fallen, Vicky thought to

herself, and it was all she could do to conceal her satisfaction that the despicable woman had finally got her comeuppance.

Maria Fernandez must have noticed. Her eyes narrowed. "You shouldn't believe everything you read in the newspapers," she said sharply. "They had to be dealt with."

"I'm sorry?" said Vicky, feigning ignorance. "I don't..."

"Oh, it is not important," said Maria Fernandez with a dismissive wave of her hand.

Vicky could scarcely believe her ears. It really was her! Not only had Augusto and Maria Fernandez been overthrown, but also, it seemed, forced into exile. Not that she had any intention of revealing what she knew. "And you ... you've come to Europe for ... a holiday?" she said.

"In a sense," came the stiff reply. She turned away. Their conversation was at an end – at least, that was what Maria Fernandez hoped.

"So, what *did* you experience in the toilet?" said Vicky.

The directness of the question caught the woman off guard. She looked up, eyes blazing. "The inside of a rat-infested prison cell," she replied. "Are you satisfied now?" She shuddered involuntarily. "And I hate rats!" she said.

Vicky gasped. "And it seemed real to you," she persisted. "Like you said about Simon..."

Maria Fernandez nodded. "More real than reality itself," she said. She paused. "It's easy to ignore reality, to take it for granted. One is unaware of so much." She looked round the carriage. "It is too warm in here. The lights are too dim. But what else?" She shrugged, and leaned forwards. "Whereas the prison cell was something else!" she whispered, her eyes wide with horror. "My senses were on fire. Every drip of water, every cry of pain, every scratch and squeak. The cold. The damp. The intolerable stench... It would not let itself be ignored." Her voice rose. "It would not let go..."

"There, there, dear," said Miss Grange as she swept back along the aisle. "Don't you go getting yourself all worked up again." She turned to Vicky, hands on her hips. "What the señora here needs most is a little bit of peace and quiet," she said sharply.

Vicky nodded. "I was just going," she said.

As she climbed to her feet, Maria Fernandez looked up. "I don't know why I told you all that," she said. Her thin lips stretched into a smile. "But I'm glad I did."

Vicky hesitated. She didn't know what to say. What was she now, a social worker? A counsellor? Personal confidante to the wife of an ex-dictator?

"Yes, thank you, dear," said Miss Grange to Vicky. She turned to Maria Fernandez cheerfully.

"You'll be pleased to hear that I didn't leave them on the sideboard after all."

"Pardon?" said Maria Fernandez wearily.

"The photographs I was telling you about," said Miss Grange, ignoring the obvious lack of enthusiasm. She placed the heavy album on the table in front of her. "Of my nephews and nieces. And my godchildren..."

Vicky turned away. The train was hurtling along the tracks now, bumping and bucking like a switchback ride, and it was so hot in the carriage that the scorched air seemed to shimmer like liquid. She felt uncomfortable, dizzy. Everything was swimming. She wiped her brow and set off up the aisle towards hers and Darren's seats.

"That's me with cousin Clarry," Miss Grange was saying behind her. "It's Clarissa really, but everyone calls her Clarry. It's she who's meeting me at the station."

"Really?" said, Maria Fernandez, stifling a yawn.

Vicky stumbled on, clutching tightly to the handrails as the speeding train jolted and jerked. She passed Mandy and Greg, who were now kissing noisily, and Simon, with his head still down on the table, staring twitchily out of the window. And all the while Maria Fernandez's words echoed round her head.

It would not let itself be ignored. What a weird thing to say. *It would not let go!*

The windows reflected back the gloomy carriage, while beyond it, the darkness glowered menacingly. Despite the heat, Vicky shivered with dread.

Darren greeted her with a raised eyebrow. "Well?" he said.

Vicky slipped in beside him. "You'll never guess who she is," she whispered.

Simon hadn't said a word since he'd sat down – not that he hadn't wanted to. He would have liked nothing better than to turn to the others and talk over what had happened. They could all have made light of it; had a good laugh … but the fear that the visions might return held him back.

It had all been so intensely real. Even now the memory of the blaze was so strong that, every time his mind wandered, he could feel the flames lapping at his skin, and he kept reaching round nervously to check that he wasn't on fire again.

The fact that it was so hot wasn't helping. He straightened up and looked round for a window he might open. But there were none in the carriage, and the air coming through the broken air-conditioning vents was like the blast from a hot oven.

Yet there was something else, beside the heat in the carriage, that niggled at him. Something he couldn't will himself to forget. He let his head slump back down on to his arms and continued staring, unblinking, out through the window.

It had all happened years ago. He couldn't remember the last time he'd thought of it, yet at the time the incident had dominated his life.

Five years earlier, it was. Simon had been sold the Victoria Warehouses in Limehouse. His understanding was that he could demolish the buildings and sell the land on. Unfortunately, after the deal had gone through and the money had changed hands he discovered that all six warehouses were in fact listed buildings. Not only was he not allowed to pull them down, but he also became responsible for their upkeep.

And so, he had come up with a solution. Having insured the buildings, he'd had them burned down. Of course, there was an enquiry, but nothing could be proved and Simon collected the money from the insurance company and then sold the land off for a massive profit, just as he'd always intended. It set him up for life.

It should have been a victimless crime. But Simon knew that was not how it had turned out. Someone had died. Terry Armstrong.

Simon shivered with guilt.

Terry Armstrong had been the nightwatchman, employed to guard the empty warehouses. Paid a pittance, he was, but having been laid-off from his previous job he'd been happy to take any work he could find. To support his family. His wife and five boys...

Simon shivered again, despite the terrible heat. Although he'd known at the time that a nightwatchman would be inside the central warehouse, he hadn't given him a second thought.

When the fire started, Terry had tried to escape. But the doors were all locked. Simon hadn't wanted anyone to raise the alarm before the fire caught hold. The policeman on the scene, suspicious of the warehouses' owner, had described to Simon how the fire had burned the man's clothes, his hair, his skin...

"Can you imagine how how hot it must have been? How every choking breath must have scorched his lungs? The absolute terror of being burned alive?"

Simon quivered with fear. Now he did.

With a sudden jolt, the train slowed down. The lights dimmed still further. Mandy and Greg fell away from one another and giggled. Maria Fernandez pursed her lips with irritation as the photograph album dropped into her lap.

"*The* Augusto Fernandez?" Darren was saying. "But he ... *whooah*!" he gasped, as the train lurched a second time and suddenly accelerated. He looked up at Vicky and grinned. "Maybe Nick was right," he said. "If we keep on at this speed we should make up the time we lost after all."

"I hope so," said Vicky, and glanced out of the

window to see how much faster they were now travelling. Scrubby bushes and twisted leafless trees blurred past in a phantom blur of brown and grey; beyond them was a rocky landscape of boulders and pinnacles. "There's not much to see," she said.

"No, but at least we can see *something* at last," said Darren.

Vicky gasped. She'd forgotten that up until that moment there had been only empty blackness beyond the window. Now that the light in the carriage had become so dim, however, the desolate scenery outside was finally visible. Yet, as she looked more closely, her heart began beating faster than ever.

"Where are we?" she said. "It looks so ... unfamiliar."

Darren turned and peered out through the glass. As the dead trees grew fewer and farther between, they found themselves passing through a harsh barren land with jagged outcrops of rock and smoking craters, swirling with a thick brown mist. Far away on the horizon, zig-zag mountains were silhouetted against the blood-red sky.

"I... I don't know," said Darren uneasily.

"It looks like the surface of the moon," said Vicky. "No, it doesn't – it looks like those pictures of the earth at the beginning of time. Volcanoes. Earthquakes. Molten lava..."

The mist grew denser, obscuring all but the

tallest pinnacles. "Maybe it's a trick of the light," said Darren. He looked round. "The street lamps of a distant town, maybe. And look how the bulbs in the carriage are flickering."

But Vicky shook her head.

"LOOK! LOOK!" screamed a voice from the other side of the carriage. It was Simon Droy. He was standing up and gesticulating wildly out through the window.

Mandy and Greg spun round; Maria Fernandez and Miss Grange looked up from the photograph album. The lights in the carriage grew brighter by degrees.

"What?" Greg demanded.

"Out there," said Simon. "Outside!"

But even as he was speaking, the dense cloud beyond the window thickened further and, as the light in the carriage continued to brighten, so the outside abruptly disappeared from view. The window became a mirror once more and they all found themselves staring at their own reflections.

Greg turned to Simon. "Seen something else, have you?" he said scornfully. "What was it this time? Witches on broomsticks? Ghostly ghoulies?"

Simon ignored him. "Didn't anyone else see what was there?" he asked, looking round desperately.

Miss Grange shook her head. Maria Fernandez turned away.

"What did *you* see?" asked Vicky uncertainly. With the thick fog obliterating everything from view, she felt more hemmed in than ever.

"See?" said Simon, his eyes rolling. "What did I see? I saw right into the bowels of fiery hell!"

Vicky's skin prickled with terror. She turned to Darren. The next instant, the silence was shattered by the sound of Greg's uproarious laughter.

"The bowels of fiery hell!" he spluttered. "Now I've heard everything!"

Even Maria Fernandez couldn't help but be amused.

"I'll tell you what, mate," Greg went on. "You've been using that mobile too much. It's cooked your brains." He turned to Mandy. "Did you hear him?"

Mandy did not respond.

"I mean, I thought he might have seen witches or ghosts – but, oh no," he said, bursting out laughing again, "he had to go and see the fiery bowels of hell!"

Mandy continued to stare at her reflection in the window. She was rubbing her left hand up and down her right bicep. Her brow was furrowed. Slowly, she began to screw herself round; her face twisted, her muscles flexed grotesquely.

Greg watched her. The smile disappeared from his face. "Mandy?" he said softly. "Mandy, what's up?"

Without showing the slightest sign that she'd

heard, Mandy opened her mouth, threw back her head and let out a blood-curdling scream. Everyone shrank back.

"Mandy!" said Greg. "Oh, Christ, not you too," he muttered. He stepped forwards and hugged her tentatively. "Mandy, it's all right," he whispered in her ear. "Believe me. It's—"

The blow from Mandy's elbow struck him viciously just below the ribs. It sent him hurtling back across the carriage and left him gasping for air.

"It can't be!" Mandy screeched. Her eyes were bulging, her mouth was frothing; she hugged her arms tightly round her body and collapsed to the floor. "N... N... Not m ... me!" she stuttered furiously, her entire body racked with violent shaking. "N... Not *me*!"

8

Mandy Hurley hadn't minded when the view outside had disappeared. For a start, she wasn't interested in what that loony, Simon Droy, might have seen; more importantly, it gave her an excuse to check her appearance.

She leant forwards and pouted.

Lippy could do with a bit of touching up, she thought. That Greg! He's got a mouth on him like a Hoover attachment. Her eyes twinkled back at her. Still, could do a lot worse, she thought light-headedly.

But then so could he! She stood back to admire herself fully. The lycra vest and cycle shorts hugged her sculpted body like a second skin, showing off her well-defined muscles to maximum effect. There wasn't an ounce of fat anywhere, she noted with pleasure.

She raised her left hand and felt her right bicep tensing as she rubbed it thoughtfully up and down, up and down. *How dare they drop you from the squad?* The words came as if from nowhere. Yes, she thought, anger rising within her. How dare they? She'd just completed the four hundred metre hurdles in under fifty-four seconds. A little more training and she might have broken the world record – not that the result would ever have found its way into the record books.

"Bastards," she muttered under her breath.

Despite all the precautions she'd taken and all the money she'd paid for drugs guaranteed not to show up in the blood or urine, the random dope test had proved positive. Not only had her run been discounted, not only had she been stripped of her medal – but she was given a seven-year ban.

Seven years!

It meant missing the next Olympics – and the one after that. Her hopes and dreams were shattered. The officials might just as well have stabbed her in the back and been done with it.

Yet Mandy Hurley had not given up. She was not the kind. Fired by the same determination that had seen her reach success in the athletics stadium, she had carved out a new career for herself. She took up bodybuilding and modelling – a combination which proved both good for her ego and her wallet.

And as for the chemical help – well, so what if it was drugs which had brought out the best in her body? She looked at her reflection lovingly, twisting round till she was side-on to the window, tensing her legs, flexing her biceps. Pose after pose, she struck, unaware of the curious gazes she was attracting from the other passengers.

You don't get a body like that from banana and raw-egg milk shakes, she thought, smirking with pride. Just look at the muscle tone! Look at the... She gasped. "What the...?"

Abruptly, the scene had changed. The train window had disappeared. In its place was a broad wall mirror. Behind her was a second mirror, so that she could see her front and her back simultaneously. All round her, huge chrome weightlifting contraptions glinted in the stark light.

"A gym?" she murmured. "How can I possibly be in a gym. I'm on a train, heading for Scotland."

She squeezed her eyes shut and counted to ten, hoping that when she opened them she would find herself back in the buffet car once again.

"...eight, nine, ten," she muttered and looked round. She frowned. She was still in the gym. There were the exercise bikes, the running machines, the free-weights. But how?

Her heart began to pound with fear; her scalp

prickled, beads of sweat broke out above her top lip. Was she dreaming? Was she going mad? Her confused reflection continued to stare back at her and, as her gaze travelled up and down her body, she saw that it wasn't only her surroundings which had changed.

"M... My b ... body," she stammered. "What's happening to my body?"

Her biceps were bulging bigger than she had ever seen them; her thighs expanded, her six-pack stomach began to writhe as if half a dozen tennis balls were moving around beneath the skin. And the pain! From the tips of her toes to the top of her head, her entire body was seized with racking cramps that twisted her this way and that.

"Wh... What's going on?" she grimaced.

Acne erupted all over her face, red and weeping. The whites of her eyes turned yellow. Her tongue hurt. Her bones ached. Hair sprouted from her legs and forearms, while that on her head turned lifeless and dull, and started to fall out. She felt giddy, she felt like throwing up. One moment she was gripped by depression, the next, she was overwhelmed by an all-consuming rage.

"Oh God," she roared. "This can't be happening. Not here. Not now. It's..." Her whole body went into spasm. Her muscles knotted; her head jerked backwards. She let out a terrible scream.

It was as though her body had abruptly ceased to

be her own. She had no control over it as it writhed and bucked. The muscles bulged, the skin strained and...

"No, no..." she gasped.

The sight of the small tear that appeared on her right thigh filled her with sudden, heart-stopping terror. The skin had split, and she was left staring down at a long, and lengthening, expanse of bulging raw flesh. She covered it with her hand, trying to pinch the gaping skin back together again.

Then she heard a ripping sound close to her ear. In the reflection, she saw a second tear which extended down her neck and across her back. The skin peeled away to reveal the muscles and tendons beneath. A third and fourth tear, and her biceps split open. Followed by the triceps and the deltoids. Within seconds, it was like looking at one of those old anatomical paintings of the human body beneath the skin.

"Help me," Mandy groaned. Her voice sounded unfamiliar. Deep. Hoarse. Bewildered.

The mirrors clouded over and darkened.

"Help you?" came the taunting reply, followed by the sound of raucous laughter. "Help *you*?"

Suddenly, she felt hands all over her, scraping painfully against the exposed flesh. She screamed and lashed out. "Leave me alone!" she screeched.

But the hands would not leave her alone. They

gripped. They pummelled. They pinched her body and wrenched at her mouth. Then one, stronger than the others, penetrated her chest. The petrified scream froze in Mandy's throat as she felt the bony fingers seize her heart and squeeze tightly.

"C... Can't b ... br ... breathe," she grunted.

The hand gripped all the more firmly, squeezing the very life out of her. Blind terror hammered inside her head. She swooned and stumbled backwards. Blackness filled her eyes. Her body collapsed to the floor, where it twitched involuntarily for ten, twenty, thirty seconds, before abruptly falling still.

"You, too," whispered the voice in her ear, and dissolved into unpleasant laughter. "Even you!"

9

"She's stopped moving!" Vicky exclaimed.

"I can see that," said Miss Grange impatiently, kneeling down awkwardly and pressing her ear to Mandy's chest. "It's all right," she said a moment later. "She's going to be all right."

"Of course she's going to be all right," came a voice behind her. It was Nick, back from behind the buffet-bar again. "If you'd just move aside," he said amiably.

He crouched down beside the motionless body still curled up on the carpet, and removed the twist of towel that Miss Grange had wedged between Mandy's jaws to stop her biting off her tongue. "It's over now," he said softly. "Look at me."

Mandy's eyes snapped opened and looked round wildly. She was on the train once more, speeding through the night. She focused in on Nick's smiling face.

"You've probably been overdoing things," he said. "Getting things out of perspective."

"Out of perspective," Mandy repeated weakly.

"Stressed up and tense." He grinned. "Leaving yourself all ... exposed."

"Tense," said Mandy. "Exposed." Her eyes opened wider and she stared miserably into Nick's understanding face. "I didn't know that..."

"Of course you didn't," said Nick. "And why should you? Don't you give it another thought."

Mandy sighed wearily and turned away. Not give it another thought? That was a laugh. She knew she would never forget what had happened so long as she lived.

"Come on, then," said Nick, holding out a helping hand. "Let's get you up off the floor and sitting comfortably. Got to make sure you're in tip-top condition by the time you arrive at wherever it is you're going, haven't we? And as soon as I've sorted out this list business, I'll open the buffet and get you something sweet to drink. Confounded red tape, eh?" he tutted. "Still, won't be long now."

As Nick helped Mandy to her feet, Vicky turned to Miss Grange. "But ... what was it?" Vicky whispered. "What happened to her?"

Miss Grange leant towards her. "She had a fit," she whispered back. "Perhaps she's epileptic. Perhaps not..."

Vicky frowned. "What do you mean?"

"Oh, I don't know," said Miss Grange, shaking her head. "I mean, look at her. A body like that. It's not natural. Who knows what she might have been taking?" She tutted. "Young people these days!"

As Nick retreated once more to the locked buffet, Greg – whom Darren had helped up – lurched back across the speeding carriage and sat down opposite Mandy, wincing with pain as he did so. He reached forwards across the table and took her hands in his own. "How's it going?" he said.

"All right," she replied without looking up.

Greg nodded. "I'll tell you what," he said. "That was one helluva blow you dealt me."

Mandy frowned. "Blow?" she said.

"You elbowed me," said Greg. "In the ribs." He rubbed the spot tenderly. "I wouldn't be surprised if you hadn't cracked a couple."

"I hit you?" said Mandy. She shook her head. "I don't remember." But even as she spoke, she recalled the hands all over her; hands that she thought were trying to harm her, not help her.

"A real belter," said Greg. "Could do with you on the rugger pitch," he grinned. "You'd make a superb scrum-half."

"I... I'm sorry," said Mandy. "I didn't mean...

I..." Her face crumpled as she dissolved into tears. "Oh, Greg," she said. "If you only knew what I went through just then. It was..." Then, suddenly realizing that everyone in the carriage was listening in to her every word, she sniffed and fell into embarrassed silence.

Outside, the smoky blackness smudged past the window faster than ever. Above the rattle of the wheels on the tracks the wind wailed forlornly. No one noticed anything outside, however, neither the sight nor the sounds. All attention focused on Simon Droy as he spun round to face Mandy.

"It was *what*?" he demanded.

"Oh, nothing," said Mandy. "It's over now."

"*What's* over now?" Simon persisted. "What happened to you? What did you see?" His cheeks were flushed with agitation. "You must tell me!"

"Just leave me alone," said Mandy.

But Simon would not leave her alone. He climbed to his feet, he moved towards her, he stuck his face into hers. "Tell me!" he demanded.

"You heard her," said Greg, moving forwards protectively. "She doesn't want to talk about it."

Simon ignored him. "What?" he said to Mandy. "What did you see?"

Greg stood up and stepped between them. "Did you hear me?" he said.

Simon turned on him, eyes blazing. "Who's asking you?" he said. "*She* saw something. *I* saw something. I want to know if we both saw the same. Now, get out of my way," he shouted, and shoved Greg to one side.

"What is this?" Greg roared as he regained his balance. "Have-a-poke-at-Greg Day?" He strode forwards, grabbed Simon by the front of his shirt and lifted him up off the ground.

Vicky had been watching the whole situation unfold with a feeling of growing impatience. The train was still gathering speed, and growing hotter and hotter as it did so. Something was wrong – very wrong. Yet there were the two of them, Simon Droy and Greg Tolson, scrapping like a couple of schoolboys in the playground.

Nose to nose, they were shouting at each other while Mandy was on her feet now, tugging at Greg's arm and pleading with him, "Leave it, Greg. He's not worth it."

"Stop it, the pair of you!" Vicky shouted. "We need to talk. We *all* need to talk."

Out of the corner of her eye, she saw Maria Fernandez turn away.

"Yeah, well, try explaining that to the gorilla here," said Simon irritably.

"Oh, naff off, you stupid little oik!" Greg bellowed, and he tossed Simon back along the aisle.

"For Christ's sake!" Vicky said. She hurried forwards and crouched down next to Simon.

"I'm all right," he said. He shook his head. "I just wanted to talk. I..."

"I know," said Vicky. She turned on Greg, eyes blazing. "You moron!" she shouted. "You bully!"

Greg backed away, arms raised protectively and quivering with mock fear. "Don't hurt me," he whimpered.

"Oi, that's enough of that!" said Darren, leaping to Vicky's defence.

"Ooh, now I'm really scared," said Greg sarcastically.

The train jolted ferociously as it hurtled into a bend. It felt, for a moment, as if they were going to be thrown from the tracks completely. Everyone held on grimly with white-knuckled horror. One crash had been terrifying enough, now it seemed they were heading for a second.

"Jeez, we're going fast," Darren murmured.

Maria Fernandez crossed herself. Miss Grange squeezed her eyes tightly shut. As they came out of the bend, the train righted itself and a collective sigh of relief went round the carriage.

Vicky let go of her grip on the seat and returned her attention to Simon. "Give me a hand here," she said to Darren.

"Coming," he said and, clutching on tightly as the train hammered on, he made his way down the aisle.

"I'm all right," said Simon. He climbed to his

feet and slumped down in the adjacent seat. "I might even sue!" he snorted. "I've met his kind before."

Vicky turned to him. "What *did* you see?" she asked.

"Fire," said Simon simply.

"Fire?" said Vicky.

Simon nodded. "But I didn't just see it. I heard it. I smelled it. I felt it..." He shuddered at the memory. His face was pale and glistening, his eyes staring, bulging, unblinking.

"You don't have to talk," said Vicky gently.

"But I want to," said Simon, fixing her with that same unblinking stare. "I... I was in this warehouse – not on the train at all – and ... and ... there was a voice on my mobile – except it wasn't a mobile, it was a torch. And ... and then the whole lot just went up in flames. It was so *real*..." He held his head in his hands. "So horribly, horribly real..."

Vicky remembered what Maria Fernandez had said about the prison cell and the rats she detested so much.

"Are you afraid of fire?" she asked.

"I am now!" said Simon. He laughed humourlessly.

"But before," Vicky persisted. "Did something happen to you when you were a child, or..."

"Look, why don't you just quit the cod psychology," said Simon, turning on her angrily.

Vicky flinched. "I... I'm sorry," she said. "I just

thought – hoped – that there might be some rational explanation for all this. I didn't mean..."

"No, *I'm* sorry," said Simon. It was guilt that had made him angry, he knew that. He'd hoped that Mandy had seen fire, too. If she had, then perhaps his own experience had been mere coincidence. He looked up. "I guess I'm just a bit shaken up still."

"That's OK," said Vicky. "I was being thoughtless."

Simon looked away awkwardly. His tongue flicked round his cracked lips. "So, when on earth is that damned buffet going to open?" he said.

Darren glanced round. The steel roller was still down and Nick was nowhere to be seen. "Haven't a clue, mate," he said.

"Well, I hope it's soon," said Simon, and smiled weakly. "I'm burning up here!"

Vicky said nothing. Yes, perhaps it was the heat in the carriage which had influenced his visions, but why had he had them in the first place? After all, she'd been unconscious when she heard voices, whereas Simon Droy had been wide awake. And anyway, it had been hot in the toilet cubicle too, yet Maria Fernandez's prison cell had been clammy and cold.

At the other end of the carriage, Greg was feeling good about himself. He'd been mortified when Nick had sent him flying back through the air, and still more embarrassed when Mandy had done the same. There was no way he was going to let it happen a third time.

He nodded towards the table where Vicky, Darren and Simon were seated.

"They're all mouth," he said to Mandy. "I knew they would be."

"I like a man who can handle himself," said Mandy.

"You have to, don't you?" said Greg. "If boarding school didn't teach me anything else, it taught me that! No one else is going to look after you." He turned back to Mandy. "So you have to look after yourself." He smiled. "And the woman you're with."

"Oh, Greg!" Mandy purred.

Greg beamed. Oh, yes, he was feeling very good about himself.

"So do you want to talk about what happened?" he said. "With me?"

Mandy turned away. "It was horrible, I..." She shuddered.

"You don't have to," he said.

"No, I... I'd like to. But you mustn't tell anyone else," she said. "I feel so embarrassed about it all."

Greg nodded understandingly.

"I was in this gym," said Mandy. "With weightlifting apparatus, mirrors..."

"Did you recognize it?" Greg interrupted.

Mandy shrugged. "One gym's much like another," she said. "I was doing warm-up exercises, striking poses, you know, in front of the mirror, when ... when..." Her face crumpled. Tears welled up in the corner of her eyes.

"In your own time," said Greg softly.

"Then everything went wrong. My face broke out in spots. My eyes turned yellow. My whole body ached." She swallowed. "And... And then I started growing hair all down my arms and legs ... and going bald at the same time. And angry! I've never felt so angry before!"

Greg shifted around in his seat awkwardly. It wasn't the first time he'd heard of such symptoms. Rick Davenport, the rugby team's number eight, had described something very similar. His eyes narrowed thoughtfully as he looked at the well-defined muscles of Mandy's shoulders and arms.

"Do you take steroids?" he asked.

Mandy lifted her head and returned his look. "Yes," she said simply.

"But ... I thought you were a hurdler? Surely you're not allowed to..."

"Used to," Mandy butted in. "I used to hurdle. Now I'm a professional bodybuilder," she said.

Greg pulled away. "Anabolic steroids," he said. "Doesn't that make you a bit ... you know ... *manly*?"

Mandy giggled. "It's all right, Greg," she said.

"You haven't been snogging a bloke, I can promise you that." She smoothed down her lycra top. "I'm all woman."

Greg smiled uncertainly. "Glad to hear it," he said.

"Anyway, I don't have a choice," she said. "I've given up athletics and I was damned if I was going to become a secretary. Or a li–*brar*-ian," she added, scornfully. "If you've got it, flaunt it, that's what my mum always used to say."

"And Mum knows best, eh?" said Greg, with a grin. He leant forward and wiped the tears from her cheeks.

Mandy smiled back at him, and sniffed. "I guess I do worry about the side-effects." She reached up and grasped his hand. "You won't tell the others, will you?"

"What, that lot?" said Greg. He shook his head. "No. My lips are sealed."

Mandy let go of his hand and traced her finger across his mouth. "That's a pity," she said.

Greg smirked. He thought of his bag on the rack by the door, and the champagne in its chiller and the two long-stemmed glasses all gift-wrapped inside it, waiting for his arrival at the station where Melissa would be.

"Penny for them!" said Mandy.

"I ... errm..." Greg said. With the temperature in the carriage so high, the champagne was bound to be warm by the time they arrived in Scotland, chiller or no chiller. He grinned lopsidedly. "Just wait here," he said, and jumped up. "I won't be a minute."

As Mandy watched Greg lurching his way down the carriage, her thoughts returned to the incident in the gym. She hadn't told him everything that had happened, cutting her tale short before she reached its terrible conclusion. Now, those final moments – when the life had been squeezed out of her heart – came back to her with such intensity that she was left gasping all over again.

It's all right, she told herself, yet the misgivings remained. The pain that had gripped her felt just as she imagined a heart attack would and, with that realization, came the memory of the newspaper item she'd read the week before.

Two athletes – Calvin Willis and Lizzie Farnham – had died in two separate incidents, brought together by the journalist under the heading, DRUGS CLAIM TWO VICTIMS. Mandy had known them both.

When her athletics career came to such an abrupt halt and Mandy had taken up the bodybuilding and modelling, she had decided to remain in touch with her old teammates. And not just so they could get together to reminisce. Calvin, a sixteen-year-old with a promising career in the triple-jump, and

Lizzie, only fifteen and already junior shot-put champion, were two of them.

Every month, she would supply them and others with the drugs to help them succeed in their chosen pursuits. Drugs to build their muscles, and to increase their speed and power. It wasn't her fault that they hadn't sought out medical advice. She wasn't to blame for their deaths.

"They begged me," she muttered, and chewed nervously at her nails. "I had no choice."

Yet even as she tried to persuade herself of her innocence, she knew she was lying. She had recognized the tell-tale signs of steroid abuse: the acne, the yellow eyes, the hurting tongue and aching bones. But she had done nothing, and dismissed their fears. Now she understood just how frightened they must have been.

"They're just side-effects," she'd told them. "They'll clear up. And think how well you're going to perform at the next big event."

Except there wasn't a next big event for either Calvin or Lizzie. They had both died of massive heart attacks.

As he strode up the carriage, Greg stared back levelly at each of the passengers as they glanced round to look at him. In their faces he saw that look of hatred and respect he'd come to recognize so well; it was a look he'd seen a thousand times before.

Bryce and Taylor Stationery Ltd had been going down the tubes before Greg Tolson had been taken on as general manager. The workforce was old and complacent and the products nondescript. It had taken him just under a year to turn things around.

First, he took a close look at the competition – filching various ideas from them – and got design and developments to come up with several new ranges of eye-catching products. Then, he stripped away the dead wood from the company, sacking anyone who would not or could not match his rigorous demands for efficiency, loyalty and productivity, and brought in a new, more compliant work-team.

His desk was situated in a glass-walled cube he'd had constructed at the centre of the open-plan office. It afforded him a view of all his employees – and woe betide anyone he caught slacking. Tea breaks and wee breaks were strictly monitored and anyone caught leaving for home before him received a black mark next to their name.

Messrs Bryce and Taylor were, of course, overjoyed with the changes that Greg Tolson had effected. They were able to pay off their debtors, invest in new machinery and pay their shareholders a handsome dividend. Greg's most recent salary cheque had been bumped up by a £10,000 bonus. It made everything worthwhile: the whispered comments, the sullen glances, the silent curses lurking behind the smiled *good mornings*. The Porsche was just one of his many new acquisitions.

As he lurched his way along the aisle of the speeding train, Greg first passed the two older women on his right. They both glanced up without interrupting their conversation.

"Have you *any* idea how much longer this journey will take?" Maria Fernandez was asking.

"Your guess is as good as mine," Miss Grange replied.

Greg grimaced. Only the week before, he'd sacked a man for coming out with just such words.

He continued towards the luggage rack, the bag, the champagne; swinging, ape-like, from handhold to handhold. He glanced dismissively at Simon as he approached, and Vicky, seated at the same table. A moron, she'd called him. A bully. And then that yob of a boyfriend leaping to her defence. Pathetic, the whole lot of them!

Just then, the train gave an almighty jolt. Greg's hand was torn away from the handrail and he was thrown down to the end of the carriage.

His arms flailing wildly at the air for something – anything – to hold on to. But there was nothing there. No rails. No racks. No seats.

Nothing at all.

It was all a blur. Even his thoughts were in a

whirl. What had made the train jolt so violently? What did he look like as he staggered and stumbled? What must the others be thinking?

The train continued to lurch and judder; first one way, then the other. He stumbled. Lost his balance. Suddenly the floor was rising to meet him. Automatically, Greg raised his hands to break his fall and slammed down heavily and painfully on his hands and knees. His back jarred, his jaws clenched, his eyes screwed shut, yet he did not cry out.

He heard birdsong. He smelled sweetly scented flowers. The sense of hurtling movement had gone.

"What the...?" he muttered.

He opened his eyes. Beneath him was a thick-pile floral carpet, quite unlike the carpet on the train. The hairs at the back of his neck tingled with fear. Scarcely daring to guess what else he might see there, he looked up – and gasped.

There was patterned paper on the walls; there were ruched curtains at the window and built-in cupboards with louvred doors lining the walls. A pink counterpane, strewn with satin scatter cushions, covered a king-size bed. Glass vases of white carnations on lace doilies stood on either side of the bed on matching bedside tables.

"Where the hell am I?" he bellowed.

10

Even as he asked, Greg Tolson knew that the answer to his question was both very simple and totally inexplicable. He climbed to his feet and had a closer look round. He was up on the first floor of a modern, suburban house in a large bedroom which had been far too fussily decorated for his liking. *That* was where he was.

"But how?" he murmured. "Where's it come from? What's happened to the train?"

Suddenly, the expression on Maria Fernandez's face when she'd emerged from the toilet came back to him; and the way Simon Droy had thrashed desperately at the empty air; and the terror in Mandy's eyes as she had recoiled from something only she could see. Now, despite everything he'd said about 'nutters', it was happening to him, too. He was standing in the middle of a fussy, feminine bedroom, so real that he could feel the warm breeze in his face and the thick carpet beneath his feet.

"It can't be happening," he groaned, and rubbed at his eyes. "I'm on a train. I'm heading for Scotland..."

Yet the unfamiliar bedroom would not let itself be ignored. A digital alarm clock pulsed the seconds from one of the bedside tables. 10.33.20 ... 21 ... 22... There was a towel on the floor. A freshly ironed shirt on a hanger hung from the key of one of the wardrobe doors. And he ... he was naked!

"What the...?" he exclaimed, spinning round nervously.

Children's voices floated in through the open windows. Two girls. A boy. The lace curtains fluttered in the warm breeze. "Come on, Daddy," the children called.

"Yes, do hurry up, Michael," urged a fourth voice, a woman's voice.

Greg crossed the room and was just about to pull the curtains aside to look outside when he noticed something gleaming – in his hand.

He was holding something.

"A knife," he gasped.

It was heavy, yet well-balanced. The handle was made of bone and bronze; the blade, of stainless steel, glinted along the length of its jagged edge.

Greg raised it to his eyes, fascinated by the mesmerizing slivers of light as they danced through the air. It was as if the glittering brilliance was shining, not on to the knife, but from it.

What *was* he doing in this strange bedroom, fresh from a shower and clutching a hunting knife? The voices outside grew more impatient.

"Come *on*!" they cried. "Or we'll go without you."

"Coming!" he found himself responding, but in a voice he didn't recognize as his own. It was whiny, high-pitched and quavering with a nervous excitement matched by his pounding heart.

All at once, the knife gave a sudden jerk. Greg let out a cry of alarm. It was the knife that had moved. Not him.

But no! he told himself. It isn't possible. It must have been...

It did it again. This time there was no doubt. The knife had moved of its own accord, slicing through the air in a wide arc and dragging his hand with it. Then, with a third movement, the knife flashed past his eyes, only millimetres away.

Breathless with sudden terror, Greg tried to open his hands and let the knife drop harmlessly to the ground. But he could not do it. He could not release the grip round the bone handle; he could not prise his fingers loose.

Again, his arm was abruptly dragged this way

and that as the knife's curious slashing dance started up once more.

"Too late!" the children outside began to chant. Over and over. "Too late! Too late! Too late!"

"Wh... What?" Greg murmured. "I don't..."

Just then, the knife seemed to become immensely heavy. Despite his own strength, Greg found himself being forced downwards. He fell to his knees. The knife, as light as a feather once more, twisted round. The light from the vicious blade flashed in his eyes as it darted down and – *thwwwp* – sliced through the soft skin just above his left wrist.

For a moment, nothing happened. Then, as the wound abruptly gaped open, blood from the severed artery gushed out across the flowery carpet. Deep red and oddly thick, it pumped out with every beat of his thumping heart.

"No!" Greg screamed. "What have I done?" He looked around blindly for the towel to staunch the bleeding. Yet even as he did so, he knew that the knife had not yet completed its work.

Once again, Greg tried to release his grip on the knife, to throw it out of harm's way. But in vain. It wrenched his arm up, leapt into the other hand, now dripping with blood. And, as Greg looked on in helpless terror, it twisted round and slashed his right wrist. A second jet of blood shot out across the carpet.

The knife, its work finally done, slipped from Greg's hand and landed, point down, on the floor — where it swayed from side to side.

"Oh God! Oh God!" said Greg. "What do I do? Help me. Help!"

He seized the towel and tried awkwardly to wrap it round both wrists. But it was a hopeless task. The cuts were so deep he could not staunch the bleeding. What was more, the blood he'd already lost was taking its toll.

As Greg stumbled towards the door, the wardrobes swayed and the walls swam. He fell giddily back down to the floor, inches from the bed. He felt sleepy. Weak. And so, so cold.

"What *are* you?" came a voice beside him, aggressive, taunting.

Groggily, Greg looked up. There was someone standing there, looming over him menacingly. Someone he couldn't make out. An indistinct smudge against the window, that was all, yet none the less imposing for that. It blotted out the sunlight; it silenced the breeze, the birdsong, the children's voices...

"Eh? I said, what *are* you?" the voice repeated. And this time it was his own voice he heard. His real voice. "And look at the state of this place."

"I... I'm sorry," Greg whispered weakly. The blood was seeping through the towel and dripping down on to the carpet. He hung his head.

"Sorry?" the voice said. "It's a little bit too late for sorry, isn't it?"

"But it isn't... It can't be," Greg groaned.

Too weak now to pull himself up on to the bed, he lay himself down on the carpet and curled up into a ball, with his throbbing wrists pressed tightly to his stomach. The blood continued to flow, warm and sticky, draining away his fear and horror and leaving him feeling completely numb.

All round him, the room began to spin. The ruched curtains and lacy frills danced and melted and, as the soft carpet seemed to swallow him up, so his vision darkened and blurred. Finally, his eyes grew heavy, and closed.

"Why?" he murmured softly.

11

"Why," said Miss Grange, pulling her ear away from Greg's mouth. She looked round at the others, now clustered about her. "He said *why*. I'm sure of it. He must be coming round."

When Greg had first begun acting so strangely, it was Evelyn Grange who had come to his aid – Mandy hadn't noticed, while the others had all remained glued to their seats. If not exactly gloating, they were certainly not sorry to see that loud bully-boy Greg Tolson was getting a taste of the horrors he'd previously sneered at so dismissively. When he'd collapsed and rolled up into a ball, however, even they had been intrigued to see what was going on.

"What do you think he saw?" Simon Droy murmured.

Maria Fernandez shuddered. Remembering her own experience all too clearly, she shook her head as she looked at his trembling body. "Something terrible," she said, "that only he understands."

Greg opened his eyes and looked up. The faces of the other passengers seemed to bounce in front of him like helium-filled balloons. He blinked. The balloons became faces. Proper faces. Concerned faces. His eyes fixed on those of Miss Grange.

"Why?" he said again, and was relieved that it was his own voice he heard, not the high-pitched whine he'd spoken in when ... when... He clutched his wrists and looked down in a sudden panic.

"I'd get him up off the floor if I were you," came a cheerful voice. "I'm sure he's all right now."

Everyone looked round to see Nick hurrying down the aisle of the train with a bundle of papers clutched in his thin, bony fingers. "Blocking the exit constitutes a breach of Network Railways by-laws," he added hurriedly, and was gone.

"Well, really!" said Mandy Hurley, who had suddenly realized what had happened and rushed over. "Talk about insensitive."

"My thoughts entirely," said Miss Grange. "And as a retired nurse with over forty years' experience, I would say that our steward is seriously underestimating the effects of the train crash on his passengers."

"What do you mean?" said Simon.

"She means we're hallucinating, don't you?" said Greg, climbing from the floor. "Having visions. Because..." He sat down heavily on the adjacent seat and wiped the back of his hand across his brow. "Because we're in shock."

"That's what *you* said earlier," said Vicky to Darren, and shivered at the memory of that awful moment when the crash had ripped through the carriage, shaking the floor and shattering the air.

"Well I, for one, thought my time was up!" said Mandy.

The others nodded.

Simon Droy chuckled. "I can sense a lawsuit coming on," he said. "You know, if we can prove the mental distress we've all suffered then we could sting Network Railways for hundreds of thousands. Maybe millions."

"Unless the train really is haunted," said Maria Fernandez, clutching at the gold cross around her neck.

Greg turned to her, his eyebrows raised.

"Yes, yes," she said. "I heard what you had to say about the *haunted toilet*. But just because..."

Greg cut her short. "I think you might be right," he said.

The others trembled uneasily. Even though Greg's behaviour earlier was both obnoxious and boorish, there had been something oddly reassuring about having someone so bluntly sceptical in their midst. His admission now, served only to heighten their own anxieties.

"You mean a ghost?" said Simon.

Maria Fernandez looked round, her dark eyes narrowed. "Ghost. Ghoul. Malevolent spirit... *Something* is not right here!"

Greg shuddered and rubbed his wrists. "You can say that again."

Outside, the great billowing folds of fog pummelled at the windows like giant cats' paws, as the train hurtled on into its dense, rolling darkness. Occasionally, it would thin for an instant, turning flimsy, like lace curtains. It offered tantalizing glimpses of the landscape beyond – a barren plain dotted with vast, towering rocks silhouetted against the brown sky like a gathering of countless terrible monsters. But then the fog would grow dense again, and the rocks would disappear.

Darren leant forward. "What *did* you see?" he said.

"Me?" said Greg. He shook his head. Where should he start? And more importantly, how much did he want to reveal? "I... I was in a strange bedroom," he said. "Flowery. Lacy. Kind of like your parents' bedroom..."

"*Was* it your parents' room?" said Vicky.

"No," said Greg. "But similar. You know, old-fashioned. Middle-aged..."

"And you'd never seen it before," Vicky persisted.

"No, never," said Greg. "And then ... then..." He winced as the memory of what happened next came back to him. "Then I was holding this knife."

Miss Grange nodded. "You shouted out something about a knife."

"That's true," said Simon. "What sort of knife was it?"

"A hunting knife," said Greg. He held his hands apart. "So long," he said. "Bone handle. Greased blade. Jagged edge. I..." he looked up at Simon. "It was so real. I could feel its weight." He paused. "I could feel the breeze coming in through the window. Hear the birds singing outside..."

"It was the same with me," said Mandy. "It wasn't as if I was dreaming or hallucinating or whatever... The touch. The smells. I remember hearing a phone ringing in the distance. Everything was so real – as real as this."

Vicky caught Maria Fernandez's eye. Everyone's stories, though different, bore the same familiar pattern. Was the señora right? Could some evil presence be responsible for what was taking place? She pursed her lips. No. Such things were the subject of books and films, not real life.

"And?" said Darren. "This knife..."

Greg hung his head. "I... I slit my wrists," he said softly. "There... There was blood everywhere. I passed out."

There was a sharp intake of breath by all the

passengers as they remembered how Greg had lain there on the floor, his hands pressed to his stomach, moaning softly. Now they knew why.

It was Miss Grange who spoke first. "I take it you had not previously been feeling suicidal," she said.

"Not at all," said Greg. He glanced up at Mandy and smirked. "If fact quite the opposite."

"And before the journey," Miss Grange persisted. "Have you ever..."

"No!" said Greg hotly. "I think it's the most contemptible action any person can commit. Cowardly..." He paused. Icy shivers were darting up and down his back. "Selfish," he murmured. "Weak..."

With a sudden jolt, Greg realized that although he had never contemplated killing himself, he knew of someone who had. What was more, the man had actually gone ahead and done it. A little over a year earlier he'd topped himself, at home, in his bedroom – and with a knife.

Gavin Smedley, his name was. He'd been a section-manager at Bryce and Taylor's. And the moment he remembered the name, Greg also knew, with absolute certainty, that it was his whiny voice he had heard in the bedroom.

Of course, he'd known Smedley was unstable from the first time they'd been introduced: he'd only kept him on at all because he understood the man had a family to support. The news, when it came that blustery Monday morning, was no surprise.

Mr Bryce and Mr Taylor had initially been concerned, fearing that Smedley's wife's accusations of bullying at work might be taken seriously. It would be a shame if the profits from the firm's recent upturn in business were frittered away in court costs and damages. But Greg Tolson's letter to her solicitor had nipped any action in the bud. Since then, he hadn't thought of the incident again – until now.

Was it possible that Gavin Smedley's ghost could have come back to him? Could it really have been Gavin Smedley's bedroom that he had seen? His knife that he had felt in his hands?

Shuddering involuntarily, he remembered the empty despair he had felt, and the words of the voice that had continued to taunt and torment – *his* words, *his* voice. And he remembered the pull of the knife as it drew the vicious blade across his exposed wrists.

"No," he trembled. "No. A person must be responsible for his or her own actions."

"My point entirely," said Simon.

Greg looked up, surprised. The conversation had clearly gone on without him. Now he had been dragged back into it.

"I still think it's something to do with the crash,"

said Miss Grange. "Shell-shock we used to call it," she said. "I remember my father when he came back from the war. Forever lapsing back into the past, he was, imagining he'd been shot, or gassed, or blown to smithereens..."

"Post-Traumatic Stress Disorder, it's called now," said Simon Droy. He rubbed his hands together gleefully. "We play our cards right, and we're going to make a killing. I'm telling you."

Darren laughed. "So, that's it, then, is it?" he said. "We're flipping out, one by one, because we all thought we were going to die in the crash." From the tone in his voice it was clear that he was far from convinced. "Either that, or the carriage is possessed!"

"Unless you've got a third possible explanation," said Simon.

Darren shrugged. "Well, perhaps you all just fainted because it's so blasted hot."

"Yeah, why don't they do something about the air-conditioning?" said Simon Droy angrily.

"It's that damned steward's fault," said Greg. "Lazy. Incompetent..."

This time no one seemed about to disagree. As Network Railways' representative, Nick was rapidly becoming the focus of everything that they considered wrong with their journey and, as the train rattled on, the disparate group of passengers became increasingly united.

"Quite useless," said Miss Grange. "He can't even get the buffet open."

"We're hungry," said Maria Fernandez. "We're thirsty..."

"You can say that again," said Mandy. "I'm absolutely gagging for a drink."

Miss Grange rummaged in her bag and produced a bottle of mineral water. "Would you like some of this?" she said. "It's a bit warm, I'm afraid."

"I'll wait a bit longer," said Mandy. "But thanks."

"As you wish," said Miss Grange. "I'm not sure I can." She twisted the cap off, tilted the water back into her mouth and swallowed. "Better than nothing," she said.

"All things come to those who wait, I suppose," Mandy sighed.

"Yeah, and patience is a virtue," snapped Greg. "But he really is pushing me to the edge of mine!"

"Actually, it isn't," said Maria Fernandez. "Faith, hope and charity, justice, fortitude, prudence and temperance. Not a mention of patience."

"Give me the sins any day," Simon Droy chipped in. "Nothing I like more than a little lust, followed by a nice load of sloth."

"Yeah, and a bit of gluttony wouldn't go amiss either," said Greg.

Miss Grange tutted with irritation and raised the bottle for a second swig of water.

"And I'll tell you another thing," said Greg. "There's... Oh God!" he exclaimed, and leapt up from his seat.

The bottle of mineral water had slipped from the woman's sweaty hands, bounced down on to the table and gushed out its contents. Greg was instantly soaked. The others laughed.

"It should have cooled you down a bit, at least," said Darren.

"Yeah, splash some down my back," said Mandy.

Greg laughed as he jiggled his dripping trouser legs about. He turned to Miss Grange. "They're right," he said. "You did me a favour."

Miss Grange stared back, her eyes wide, her lower lip trembling.

"Miss Grange?" said Vicky.

"She can't hear you," said Darren.

Greg moved his hand up and down in front of her unblinking eyes. Her breath was beginning to come in short, urgent little gasps.

"She's gone," he said quietly.

With no warning, the woman's eyes abruptly rolled back in her head and she began coughing furiously. Her hands clawed at the air. Her face turned red.

"My dear Miss Grange!" Maria Fernandez exclaimed. "What in heaven's name...?"

"Some water must have gone down the wrong way," said Vicky.

Maria Fernandez nodded. "Perhaps," she said. She climbed to her feet and patted Miss Grange vigorously on the back. "Come on, now," she said encouragingly. "Take a deep breath. You'll be all right."

"Look at her eyes," said Simon. "Look at the fear."

"I'm telling you, it's happening to her, too," said Greg.

"Don't just sit there," said Maria Fernandez irritably, as Miss Grange broke away from her and staggered off down the lurching carriage. "The poor woman's in obvious distress. We've got to do something to help her."

The others watched as Miss Grange continued her strange, flailing dance. Her face was blotchy now. The redness had darkened to a shocking shade of purple, while her lips were turning blue.

"But what?" gasped Maria Fernandez. "What *can* we do?"

12

It was odd, Miss Grange had been thinking when Mandy turned down her offer of a drink, that whenever you get a random group of people together, it always seems to be the same mix. The different types of women. The different types of men. The age range.

Unlike at Bevendean, that is, she mused. But then Bevendean Nursing Home for Elderly Gentlewomen hadn't housed a random group of people, but rather a group of women who had come together precisely because they were the same: old and, to varying degrees, infirm.

She stole a final glance at Mandy Hurley before turning away completely. One day, even you will be old, she thought.

That hard young body would turn flabby and slack, while her ambition – the driving force which was propelling her though life – would weaken and fade. She would become like all the others.

Miss Grange opened the bottle and took a sip. She winced. There was nothing worse than warm mineral water. Still, it was better than being thirsty. She closed her eyes and took a second, longer drink from the bottle...

"Did you remember to get the butter?" she heard Maria Fernandez saying.

She lowered the bottle and turned her head. "I beg your pardon?" she said, opening her eyes slowly. "Did you say, *butt*—?"

The word caught in her throat. Maria Fernandez was nowhere to be seen. Nor were any of the other passengers. In fact she wasn't on a train at all. Yet she was not alone.

"So this is it," she murmured, surprised that she was remaining so lucid. "My hallucination."

She looked round.

But that's strange, she thought. The others claimed not to recognize their surroundings – yet I know this place.

It was all so familiar. The vaulted ceiling. The high windows. The two rows of six beds, each with its occupant curled up and wheezing, snoring and prattling in her sleep.

She was lying on Bed 12 in Ward C of the

Bevendean Nursing Home, the place where she had worked for over forty years.

"Did you remember to get the butter?" a voice from the other end of the ward cried out. "Only I don't like margarine."

Miss Grange sighed wearily. "What must it be like," she wondered, "ending up in a place like this, head full of trivia?"

It was all too depressing. After all, she was not old; she was in late middle-age and in perfect health. What was more, thanks to her cousin, who had suggested she might like to come and help run the seaside bed–and–breakfast business, she had finally taken hold of her future with both hands. What on earth was the point, she wondered, of reliving this dreary place where she had wasted so much of her life already?

She closed her eyes. "Make it all go away," she told herself. "You are on a train. You are heading to Scotland to stay with Clarry. You are..."

She opened her left eye a fraction and looked round. "Blast!" she exclaimed.

The ward was still there. And more real than ever. She could smell that heady mixture of carbolic, vomit and bedpans. She could hear every wheeze, splutter and snore from her neighbours. She could taste the stale air.

"Only I don't like margarine!" came the plaintive voice once more.

"Oh, for Heaven's sake!" she shouted, and was horrified to find that her own voice sounded frail and cracked.

The air was filled with raucous laughter. "For *Heaven's* sake!" a strident voice cried out. "The nerve of the woman!" The cackling grew louder.

"Stop it," Miss Grange said weakly. "Stop it at once."

She closed her eyes, she clamped her hands over her ears, but she couldn't shut out either the sights or sounds of what was going on around her. And when she tried to move – simply to get up and leave the ward – she found herself strapped to the bed.

"Let me go!" she said, panic rising in her throat. "Let me out of here." She wriggled and squirmed, trying in vain to reach round to the buckle. "I don't belong here! Let me..."

The water caught her completely by surprise. It filled her eyes, her mouth. Some trickled down into her lungs, making her cough and splutter. She looked round wildly. Suddenly, there was water everywhere, crashing in from all sides. Ice cold and tasting of earth. Deeper, it got. Deeper and deeper.

"Help!" Miss Grange cried out. "Hel...! She spluttered violently as the water rose up over her head.

Eyes wide with terror, she fumbled for the strap which was keeping her pinned to the bed. She tugged it round, centimetre by centimetre, until the buckle was within her grasp. Little by little she pushed the slippery leather through the clasp. Her fingers shook. Her heart pounded. The belt fell away.

Free from her constraints at last, she rose away from the bed and floated up through the water. She pushed down with her arms, again and again, desperate to reach air as soon as possible.

Yet how far was it to the surface? How deep was the water?

She looked round in disbelief at the endless expanse of water. The ward had disappeared completely now. She was struggling up through the waters of a cold grey lake.

I've got to make it, she thought desperately, as she kicked her legs and pushed down harder with her arms. I've just got to.

But it was so, so difficult. Her wet clothes weighed her down and the coldness of the water was numbing her flesh, stealing her strength. Suddenly, her ears popped. She rose higher.

But will it be fast enough? she wondered.

Even now her entire body was screaming out for air. Her head throbbed. Her heart thudded. Oxygen. She must have oxygen. She must breathe in.

No. Cannot, she told herself. Must not...

The surface came closer. She could see the full moon through the water, wriggling above her like snakes in a pit. Any second now and she would burst from the water into wonderful, cool, clean air, and breathe; breathe as she had never breathed before. Her left hand broke the surface. Then her right hand. Then...

No! *NO!*

She thrashed around in sudden blind panic, desperate to break free of the bony hands which gripped her shoulders and held her down.

It's no good. Can't ... hold my breath any ... longer.

Just then, a ghostly face loomed up in front of her. Its face was white and bloated, its eyes were like two featureless pebbles. With a sudden gasp of terror, Miss Grange inhaled. The water gushed in through her mouth and filled her lungs.

And everything turned black.

13

"**B**reathe!" Vicky shouted. She was crouching down by Miss Grange where she had fallen. "Come on, just breathe." She looked round at the others. "Her heart's stopped," she said. "What do I do?"

Greg and Simon shook their heads dumbly. They had no idea.

"It looked as though she was choking," said Mandy.

"Choking?" said Maria Fernandez. "Drowning more like."

Vicky turned back to the motionless woman. "Is that possible?" she said. "On a slurp of water?"

"I think we must assume the answer is yes," said Maria Fernandez. "Does anyone know how to give the kiss of life?"

For a second time, Greg and Simon shook their heads.

"Darren!" said Vicky urgently. "You did that course."

"That was ages ago," said Darren. "I don't know if I can even remember how to..."

"You've got to try!" said Vicky. "It could be her only hope."

Darren stared for a moment at the woman, at her purple face and blue lips. "OK," he said. "I'll give it a go."

He rolled her over on to her back and knelt down beside her. Then, raising her head and pinching her nostrils shut, he breathed into her mouth. Four ... five ... six... He let her down, head turned to one side, and with plaited fingers pressed down on her chest. Nothing happened.

"She can't have drowned," he said. "Something else must have..."

"Try again!" said Vicky urgently.

Darren nodded grimly and repeated the procedure. Then again. And again. "This is hopeless," he said. "She..."

At that moment, Miss Grange's head snapped forward, and a gush of water exploded from her mouth. She spluttered and gasped for breath. She looked up, to the young thug with the offensive T-shirt towering above her.

"Oh, my God!" she cried. "What are you doing? Get your hands off me!"

"You're all right!" Maria Fernandez exclaimed. "We were all so worried. You blacked out."

"And ... and what?" said Miss Grange sitting up. Her face was still puffy and discoloured. She glared at Darren. "Was he ... taking advantage?"

"You what?" said Darren, pulling back sharply.

Mandy and Simon exchanged amused glances. Vicky stepped forwards.

"You don't understand," she said. "He was giving you the kiss of life. You were choking on your water. We thought you were drowning."

"Drowning," Miss Grange repeated and shuddered.

Suddenly, the hospital ward came back to her. The creaking beds, the tang of carbolic, the old women – and Lettie. Always going on about butter and margarine, she was. Incontinent. Senile. Alone...

It was intended as a kindness, she told herself as she recalled how, in the middle of the night, she had pinched her nose shut and poured the water into her throat; how she had clamped her hand over her mouth and held her down until she had stopped struggling. But it was meant for the best. The old woman's will had nothing to do with it. She'd wanted to put her out of her suffering. A quick death. A painless death...

The memory of those awful final moments came flooding back to her. The panicked thrashing. The bony hands, pinning her down. The earthy taste. The numbing coldness. The water gushing into her burning lungs. Drowning.

She *had* been drowning...

She turned to Darren. "I owe you an apology," she said without meeting his gaze.

"Yeah, well, we'll say no more about it then," said Darren grudgingly.

"Here, you!" bellowed Greg.

The others spun round to see Nick scurrying along the aisle, his head darting from side to side as he inspected under each of the tables. His lank hair was unkempt. His waistcoat was undone and his shirt was coming untucked from his trousers.

"Can you hear me?" Greg demanded.

Nick straightened up. "Perfectly, sir," he said. Despite his smile, his glistening goatee beard twitched with agitation. He glanced round at the faces of his passengers. "Everything all right, is it?" he said.

"All right?" Greg blustered. "No, it is not. We..."

"Would you like a complaint form, sir?" he said. "I'd understand if you did."

The steward's tone of helpful concern disarmed Greg completely. "No, I... Yes... It's not a question of..."

"Why have we still received no information

about the crash?" Miss Grange, back to her normal self, demanded.

"Or when we're due to arrive," added Maria Fernandez. "It's absolutely inexcusable."

"And why don't our mobiles work?" Simon Droy butted in.

"And why's it so hot?" said Vicky.

"And when are you finally going to get that damned buffet open?" said Darren.

"Yeah!" said Mandy scornfully. "Fat lot of good it was getting complimentary vouchers if we can't even use them!"

"I know, I know," said Nick. He raised one hand for quiet, while clutching on tightly with the other as the train thundered on along the tracks. "You've had a dreadful time of it," he said, "and I sympathize. Believe me!"

"That's not enough," said Miss Grange. "We don't want your sympathy. We want you to do something. Now."

Nick turned and smiled solicitously. "I know you do," he said, "and I appreciate how galling it must be for you to remain in ignorance about the cause of the crash. But, as I already told you, the intercom system is down. As is the air-conditioning," he added, looking at Vicky, "or so it would seem. And with regard to your mobile, sir," he said, turning to Simon, "I seem to recall that you did receive *one* call."

Simon blanched. "I... I can't call out," he said. "I need to let people know when I'll be arriving."

Nick nodded amiably. "I can only advise you to keep trying, sir," he said. "I'm afraid I'm not an expert in such matters. Though I can confirm that we will be arriving at our destination at the time we were due to arrive," he added, turning to Maria Fernandez, "if not a couple of minutes early."

"If we ever arrive at all!" Maria Fernandez retorted.

"Madam?" said Nick.

"I've never been on such a train before," she said. "I mean I've travelled fast before – in France for instance. But there, the trains are smooth. They glide. Not like this ... this..." She swept her arm round in a wide arc. "Just look at it."

Everyone, including Nick, looked round. The windows were rattling. The tables and seats were vibrating. The luggage in the racks, both overhead and in the stack by the door, was bouncing about as the train lurched and jolted.

"I can assure you, madam, that Network Railways' safety record is second to none..."

"Second to none!" Miss Grange broke in. "We've already had one crash this journey. Now the driver seems hell-bent on finishing the job off properly!"

Nick smiled sweetly. "It's the fog," he said. "Because you can't see anything outside, it makes our speed seem faster than it is." He beamed. "And I'm afraid fog is one thing Network Railways cannot be held responsible for."

Even as he spoke, the carriage gave an almighty lurch. Simon Droy, who had left his seat, hurtled across the aisle and landed on the table opposite. Nick, gripping hold of the handrail with white-knuckled ferocity, reached over to help him up.

"Get off me!" Simon snapped. He pulled himself up and glared at the steward. "You and the rest of Network Railways are going to regret this," he hissed. "We shan't let you forget this atrocious journey. Any of you."

Nick raised his eyebrows. "I do hope that wasn't intended as a threat, sir," he said, his voice hardening.

"No, it wasn't," said Simon, staring back evenly. "It was a promise."

Greg watched Nick's face closely, half-expecting to see those eyes glint red with rage again. Instead, the steward smiled. "What we all need is some light refreshments," he said.

"That's what I've been saying the whole journey," said Mandy. "Just open the buffet!"

"Of course," said Nick. "Just as soon as I've found that wretched list. I must tick your vouchers off. I'm afraid it's simply more than my job's worth to cut down on the paperwork. Sloppy administration can have more repercussions than any of you could ever imagine. Can't have people disappearing on a technicality, can we?" He turned away.

"Then just let us pay for the stuff," said Simon.

"Yeah, Vicky and me haven't got any vouchers anyway," said Darren. "We..."

But Nick was not listening. Head bowed once again, he was scurrying back along the aisle, peering under the remaining tables and round the snack-and-chat area.

"Where the hell is it?" they heard him muttering angrily. "Where?" He paused. "The bin-bags... Oh, surely I couldn't have been so stupid. But I'll have to check. Damn! Damn! Damn!" he cursed through clenched teeth as he stormed back to the door marked *Private*, and disappeared inside.

For a moment, no one said a word; the next, everyone was talking at once.

"He's the most creepy man I've ever met," Mandy said with a shiver of revulsion.

"Reeee-volting!" Vicky agreed.

"*Fog* indeed!" Maria Fernandez muttered indignantly. "We're travelling too fast, and that's a fact."

"Far too fast," Miss Grange said, nodding vigorously.

"And I'm still too hot," said Simon. "And too thirsty. And too hungry..."

"We're right back where we started," said Greg angrily.

"You're right," said Darren. "He's got a real way of weaselling out of things."

"Yeah, well, I've had enough," said Greg, climbing to his feet. As he did so – almost losing his balance in the process – he was struck once again by just how fast the train was travelling. "I'm going to insist he opens that door to the rest of the train," he said.

Mandy frowned. "Are you sure that's wise? You know what happened last time."

"It won't happen again," said Greg darkly, as he set off for the buffet.

Simon got up and, clutching on tightly, followed him down the aisle. Greg turned. "Reinforcements?" he said.

"Nah," said Simon. "Witness." He tapped his nose. "Every statement we make must be corroborated if..." He paused. "What was that?"

"What was what?" said Greg.

"Listen," said Simon. He cocked his head to one side. "That banging noise."

Greg frowned. "The wheels on the tracks, isn't it?" he said.

The banging and crashing started up again, followed by a torrent of muffled expletives. "It's coming from the buffet," said Simon.

The pair of them moved closer to the door and

pressed their ears against the white surface. The noise grew louder. It was definitely coming from inside. Greg pulled away and turned to Simon.

"What on earth...?" he said.

Simon shrugged. He clenched his right fist and went to knock. Greg grabbed him by the wrist.

"Hold on," he said. "Let's catch him unawares." He reached out tentatively for the door handle, realizing as he did so just how much his hand was trembling.

He turned the handle slowly, silently, and pulled. The unlocked door slid open with a blast of intense heat. Shielding their eyes, Greg and Simon peeked in through the narrow gap. Greg's jaw dropped with surprise. Simon trembled.

"Oh my God!" he muttered weakly.

The train pitched abruptly to the left. Greg pushed the door to again, and let the latch slide silently shut. He turned to Simon. "We'd better tell the others," he said.

Beyond the windows, the fog was growing increasingly patchy. Glimpses of the landscape became longer, and clearer, as they hurtled past. Vicky gasped and clutched at Darren's arm.

"Look," she said.

Darren turned. So did Miss Grange and Maria Fernandez. Even Mandy Hurley, though still nervous, turned her attention to the window. All four of them trembled with foreboding. The plains outside were as barren and rocky as before and, under the glowing blood-red sky, were now brightly enough illuminated to be seen despite the lights in the carriage.

"W...Where are we?" Miss Grange whispered.

"You mean, you don't know?" said Maria Fernandez. She sighed. "I must admit I'd thought England would be greener..."

"I've never seen anywhere like it," said Miss Grange, shaking her head. "It's so bleak. So dead! And the sky..."

The air shimmered. The rocks quivered. Spinning wisps of mist, hovering close to the ground, glided this way and that as if in some strange dance.

"I don't like it," said Mandy, turning away. "It's scary. Spooky..."

"Hey, you lot!" came a voice. The others turned to see Simon hurrying towards them as fast as the lurching train would allow. His face was pale, waxy-white and glistening with sweat.

"What's up?" said Darren, forgetting all about what he'd just seen. "You look as if you've seen a ghost."

"Worse than that," said Simon shakily.

"We've got to get out of here," said Greg. "And now!"

"Get out?" said Mandy. "But the door's locked."

"Then we break it down," said Greg.

"But…" Vicky began.

"It's Nick," said Simon.

"Nick?" said Miss Grange.

"He's gone mad!"

"You know what they say," said Darren. "You don't have to be mad to work here, but it helps…"

" No, I mean *really* mad!" said Simon. "Stark raving bonkers! He's thrashing about in there like a maniac, smashing the whole place to pieces."

"Maybe he too is suffering from delusions," said Maria Fernandez.

Greg shook his head. "It's that list he keeps going on about," he said. "He's turning the whole place over trying to find it."

"And what's worse," said Simon. "He's got a knife."

Just then, a resounding crash echoed from the buffet, followed by raging curses and a second crash, louder than the first. The seven passengers looked at one another, horrified, bewildered.

"I'm telling you," said Greg. "We're locked up in here with a complete psycho! We've got to get out. Now!"

14

As they hurried towards the door at the front end of the carriage they discovered just how fast the train was now going. It jumped and jarred alarmingly as it careered along the tracks. Behind them, the sounds of wilful destruction coming from the buffet grew louder, drowning out the clatter of the wheels.

"He's ripping the place apart," said Greg.

"Now I'm never going to get that ice-cold drink," said Mandy. She wiped the beads of sweat from her forehead.

"I don't think he ever had any intention of opening up," said Darren. "All that smiling and hand-wringing while he was dithering over the so-called list!"

"Yeah, and that guff about needing clearance to unlock the door," said Greg. "He's up to something. The question is, what?"

Simon trembled. "I, for one, am not planning on staying to find out. You should have seen him!" he told the others. "Bright red face. Snarling teeth. And his eyes! God, if looks could kill! I've never seen anyone as furious."

"And armed," Greg reminded him.

"And armed," Simon repeated, as he mopped his brow. "If he turns on us, we won't stand a chance."

Greg stopped in front of the door and gave it a cursory inspection. It was an electric slide door, with a poster glued over the glass, obscuring their view.

"We'll need something to lever it open," he said.

"I know," said Greg. "I've got a steel ruler in my brief case. Do you think…"

"Too flimsy," said Simon. "Anyway, we'll have to break the lock before we can slide the door across."

Behind them, Miss Grange rummaged through her bag. "How about this?" she said.

Maria Fernandez gave a squeak of surprise. Miss Grange blushed.

"You can't be too careful, these days," she said.

"Too right," said Mandy. "I carry mace with me. In a spray."

Greg trembled with horror as he stared at the knife in Miss Grange's outstretched fingers. He turned to Simon. "You ... you have a go," he said. "I'll try and pull the door back."

Behind them, an almighty crash echoed from the far end of the carriage. Simon grabbed the knife and rammed the blade into the crack at the edge of the door, just above the lock. Then, tensing his arms and gripping the handle, he brought it down heavily, twisting at the same time.

Nothing happened.

He had a second attempt. Then a third and a fourth. "It's no use," he said.

The others groaned. Greg slipped off one of his shoes and began hammering at the glass. "Break, damn you!" he yelled. "Break!"

"It's reinforced," said Simon. "You'll never..."

"Then give me the damned knife," said Greg.

"No, give it to me," said Mandy, taking it from Simon.

"Think you're stronger than me, do you?" said Greg.

"I'm sure I am," said Mandy with a smile. "But I wasn't going to use brute strength." She inserted the point into the lock itself. It was a double-clawed device that gripped a fixed bar. If she could just get the blade at the point where the claws crossed... She steadied her grip on the handle with both hands and pushed hard forwards. There was a click. The lock gave.

"Fantastic!" Greg shouted. "Right, then. Let's

see if we can drag the door open. It's going to be a tight squeeze, but we've all got to try and get a fingerhold in the door. Darren, Simon: you take the top of the door. I'll go in the middle. Mandy, move down a little. Vicky, there. That's it. Now, when I say pull, *pull*!"

Crushed into place, the five of them pushed their fingertips into the gap at the edge of the door. Maria Fernandez and Miss Grange looked on.

"Good luck!" they whispered.

"Pull!" shouted Greg.

As one, they tugged, necks straining, knuckles white. But the door wouldn't budge.

"Again!" said Greg. "One, two, three ... *pull*!"

Once more, they tugged with all their strength. Greg grunted with exertion. Simon groaned. Mandy's eyes glinted as her muscles tensed and bulged.

"It's moving!" Greg groaned. "Just a bit more... Pull!"

Vicky gritted her teeth and heaved all the more desperately. Though her arms were throbbing and her fingertips were numb, she was as keen as any of them to leave the terrible buffet car. It was so hot; so claustrophobic. Like being shut up inside a box, she thought and shuddered. Or a coffin...

"My fingers are slipping!" said Simon.

"We need something to stick into the gap," Greg said, his voice straining. "To keep the door from sliding back."

For a second time, Miss Grange reached into her bag. This time she pulled out a foldaway umbrella. "Will this do?" she said.

"It'll have to," said Greg. "Wedge it in."

Miss Grange leaned over Mandy and Vicky, and rammed the rolled umbrella into the narrow gap between the door and its frame. Greg released his grip on the door and stepped back. With a groan of relief, the others did the same. The umbrella held.

"Blimey," said Simon, shaking his hands vigorously. "I thought my arms were about to drop off."

Vicky mopped her brow. Mandy rubbed her throbbing muscles. Darren inspected the side of the door, running his hand up and down the rubber-padded edge and squinting into the gap.

"We still haven't reached the edge of the outer door frame," he said. "A couple more centimetres should do it though. Then we'll finally get a bit of fresh air coming in."

From the far end of the carriage, the furious banging and crashing continued.

"Come on then," said Greg. "We haven't got much time. Let's have another go."

This time, as the others took up positions at the door with their fingers wrapped round the rubber seal, Greg wedged himself against the toilet door and pushed his heel into the narrow gap. He braced himself. The others took the strain, ready for the command to pull. Sweat beaded every furrowed brow. As one, they held their breath.

"One, two, three," said Greg, "*PULL!*"

With a groan, Mandy, Simon, Vicky and Darren all yanked at the door as hard as they could. At the same time, Greg tensed his leg and pressed backwards. There was a grinding sound as the door moved slightly to the right – not far, but just far enough for them all to slide their fingers deeper into the gap and pull all the harder.

"It's moving," Darren grunted. "Pull! *Pull!*"

The door slid across a little further. The umbrella fell to the floor.

"Don't let go, any of you," Greg instructed, "or it'll slam shut again."

"Work together!" Darren cried out. "Heave! Heave! *Heave!*"

The carriage lurched and jolted. The door moved a couple of millimetres more.

"Pull harder!" yelled Greg. He glanced round at the two older women. "Find something bigger to wedge into the gap," he grunted.

"My suitcase," said Maria Fernandez. "Wait a second."

Clutching desperately on to the hand rails, she tottered back to her seat, pulled the smaller of her two hard, black cases down from the rack and returned to the end of the train.

"It's reinforced," she said. "Bomb-proof."

"Be ready to push it into place when the door's open enough," Greg grunted. Stinging sweat poured over his face, into his eyes, down his neck. "Right. One last heave. All together, *NOW*!"

Drawing on reserves of strength they didn't even know they had, they pulled as they'd never pulled before. There was a loud screech and the door lurched to one side.

Maria Fernandez, down on her hands and knees, attempted to guide the suitcase into the gap. "Just a bit more!" she called.

"Again!" Greg shouted. "We can do it!"

All at once, their efforts were rewarded with a blast of air. They'd made it past the outer door frame. Wincing against the stinging wind, Maria Fernandez tried to ram the case into the gap – but still it wasn't quite wide enough.

"I can't," Simon groaned miserably.

Below him, Mandy was having problems of her own. The way she was crouched, she was taking the full force of the searing blast of air. It scorched her face and snatched her breath away. "I'm losing my grip!" she wailed.

The door juddered.

"Quick!" yelled Greg.

Maria Fernandez hammered at the gap with her suitcase. The door trembled.

"It's shutting again!" screeched Vicky.

Instinctively, Darren kicked the case out of the

way and slammed his boot into the closing gap. The door hammered against it and remained open. The whistling wind poured into the carriage like boiling water gushing through a dam.

"Ouch!" said Greg wincing at the sight of Darren's boot trapped in the door.

"It's all right," he said. "They've got steel toecaps. Though this wind is something else!" he added and turned away from the blast, wincing.

The air rushing into the carriage was as hot as the air already there, and certainly no fresher. It smelt of factory chimneys – sooty and sulphurous. Only the fact that it was moving made it seem refreshing, cooling the tired, sweating bodies as it whistled past.

"This is quite unbelievable," said Miss Grange. She was standing away from the incoming air, fanning herself. "It's December, for pity's sake. Yet it feels like midday in the Sahara."

Vicky paled. "You don't think the rest of the train's on fire, do you?"

"On fire?" said Darren.

"Why else would the air be so hot?" she said. "Maybe the crash started a fire in the engine, and it's spreading back through the train."

Darren twisted his head back round and, shielding his eyes, peered into the gap. It was dark out there. Gloomy. The same blood-red light as before glowed down on the tracks which stretched out ahead of them. He gasped with sudden horror.

"What is it?" said Vicky.

"I... I..." Darren stammered.

"What? What can you see?"

He twisted back, unable to tolerate the tremendous force of the wind a moment longer. His eyes were streaming; the colour had drained from his face.

The others stared at him in alarm.

"*Is* it on fire?" asked Miss Grange at last.

Darren shook his head. "There ... there's nothing there to be on fire," he said.

"What?" Greg shouted incredulously, and ducked round behind Darren to see for himself.

"Nothing at all," said Darren shakily. "We're on our own." His voice was thin and trembling.

Greg turned back. He looked utterly defeated. "He's right," he whispered. "The carriage must have been uncoupled. We're out of control, hurtling along under our own momentum. Unless a miracle happens, then..."

15

No one spoke. Although Greg did not finish his sentence, everyone knew what had been left unsaid. If nothing was done quickly then they were all going to perish. Suddenly, the rattle and thud of the speeding train had become something to be feared, not welcomed.

Simon thought of the football match he would never watch. Mandy saw her dreams of becoming women's bodybuilding champion fade away to nothing. Greg, Maria Fernandez and Miss Grange all pictured the faces of those who were waiting in vain for them.

Vicky turned to Darren, hot tears trickling down her cheeks. She thought of the surprise she'd been planning to spring on Darren the following day and patted her back pocket. "Do you think we're ever going to make it to that cottage?" she whispered.

"Course we are," said Darren, smiling bravely.

"But how?" wailed Miss Grange. "We're locked up in this runaway carriage. We're never going to escape…"

"And just when I thought things couldn't get any worse," said Mandy miserably. Shielding her eyes, she peeked through the gap and stared at the gaping nothingness racing towards them. "Why are we going so fast?"

"We must be on a slope," said Simon. "A steep slope."

"But they don't build railways on slopes," said Vicky. "Do they?"

At that moment, Miss Grange's empty mineral water bottle came rolling down the aisle. It came to rest against Greg's shoe. "They must have on this occasion," he said, kicking the bottle away angrily.

"What are we going to do?" said Miss Grange.

"I haven't a clue," Greg admitted.

"Pray," said Maria Fernandez, dropping to her knees. "Pray that we come to a safe standstill."

The barren landscape blurred past the windows on either side. Brown rocks. Red sky. The pale wisps of mist dancing in the hot shimmering air.

"Brakes," said Simon.

"What?" Greg looked at him, puzzled.

"Don't individual carriages have brakes?" said

Simon. "I thought it was one of the recommendations of that Railway Report. After the Bridgewater disaster..."

"He's right," said Miss Grange. "I read about it. I'm sure I did."

Maria Fernandez looked up. "In my country, each of the carriages has an individual brake." She nodded towards the door, still held partially open by Darren's boot. "Out there," she said. "A manual lever."

Greg looked from one to the other with amazement. Talk about clutching at straws, he thought. Then again, the buffet did seem to have its own electricity supply. What if it also had an independent braking system. He realized the others were staring at him expectantly.

"What?" he said.

"Don't you think we ought to take a look?" said Darren.

"It could be our only hope," said Simon.

As the others grouped together around the door once again, Vicky pressed her face against the side window and gazed out. It was still dark, yet the red glow was growing brighter. Far, far in the distance, the sun, partially risen above the horizon, failed to move higher.

I was wrong before, she realized. It doesn't look like the earth at the dawn of time at all. It looks like a sci-fi picture from a world with a dying sun too weary even to rise...

She cupped her hands around her eyes to shut out the light from the carriage, and squinted at the landscape. Like before, she was struck by its rocky desolation. The tall boulders and vast rocky crags stood like petrified ogres and gremlins, and between them – bestowing upon them the illusion of life – were the wraith-like twisters that flitted through the misty air.

She frowned. There was something about the way they were moving...

Above her head, there came a cracking sound and a large section of the plastic covering was torn away from the ceiling.

"Duck!" Darren shouted.

Everyone covered their heads. The panel flipped over and flapped harmlessly back along the aisle. From the other end of the carriage a howl of rage went up from the buffet-bar.

"Right," said Greg, and clapped his hands together. "Let's get this blasted door open once and for all."

Darren nodded down at his trapped boot. "I'll second that," he said. "I'm getting terrible cramp."

They got into position again, fingers wrapped around the edge of the door, legs braced. Greg wedged himself back against the side wall with one foot up against the edge of the door.

"Come on, Vicks!" Darren called out impatiently. "No slacking."

But Vicky did not hear him. Spellbound by the curious spinning columns of dusty air which clustered all round the train, she could not tear herself away.

It's almost as if they're alive, she thought. They were darting this way and that, flimsy, diaphanous, mesmeric, as the carriage hurtled through them. Most coiled off to the left and right; some slid over the top, and all of them disappeared into the slipstream which sucked them back and away behind the carriage. Yet, as Vicky continued to stare, something different was happening.

They were beginning to cluster together. To merge. Suddenly, instead of knocking aside the individual dancing twisters, the carriage was hurtling through a solid wall of the dense, misty air which writhed and squirmed against the window.

"Vicky!" came an impatient voice. It was Darren again. "Will you come on!"

Vicky turned her head. At the same moment Miss Grange cried out.

"Get away from me!" she screamed. "Leave me alone!"

"What?" Greg demanded impatiently. "What now?"

Vicky spun round. She saw one of the wraith-like columns of air whirling round and round the bewildered woman. It looked more animated than ever. Eyes – she could make out eyes – and fingers stroking Miss Grange's petrified white face...

What was more, the wispy form was not alone. One by one, others were slipping in through the crack in the door. They twisted. They turned. They surrounded the hapless passengers.

"Get off!" Mandy screeched, releasing her grip on the door and thrashing wildly at the air.

Simon screamed. Greg gritted his teeth and attempted in vain to convince himself the apparitions were figments of his imagination.

"Go away!" groaned Maria Fernandez.

Despite their entreaties, more and more of the curious phantasms poured into the carriage, until the air was thick with swirling, spinning mist.

"Close the door!" Greg shouted.

"I... I'm trying," Darren shouted back. Like Greg, he could no longer convince himself that it was just the wind howling and wailing, ruffling his hair and plucking at his clothes. It sounded too much like voices. It felt too much like inquisitive fingers, inspecting, probing... Jaws clenched, he wriggled his foot round, frantically trying to pull it free.

"Come *on*!" said Greg.

"Give us a hand, then!" shouted Darren.

Wedging himself tightly against the wall, Greg raised his other leg and, with both heels now against the edge of the door, pressed back. The door shifted a fraction.

"NOW!" he bellowed.

Darren twisted his foot sharply to the right and pulled it back. There was a squeaking sound of leather on rubber. The boot came free and, with a thud, the door slammed back into place.

"Yes!" Darren shouted. "I've done it."

The next moment, his relief at being free once more shifted to absolute horror as the misty wraiths turned on the passengers. They whirled through the air, pinching and prodding, and loudly screeching – now with fury; now with malicious delight.

Darren quaked fearfully. Because he'd removed his foot from the door, they – whatever they might be – were now sealed inside the carriage. All round him, the other passengers screamed with terror. But what *could* they be, these wispy apparitions?

Ghosts? Demons? Evil spirits?

One of them twisted round his body and pressed its face close to his own. Darren recoiled and turned away, but the misty being was not deterred. Pressing its leering face close to his own, it opened its mouth to reveal a row of pointed wolf-like teeth.

"Yes," it answered softly, its foul hot breath blasting into Darren's face. "And yes. And yes again!"

Then, as abruptly as it had sought him out, the demonic spirit uncoiled itself and flew off to another victim. The sound of its raucous, cackling laughter echoed round the carriage.

"What have I done?" Darren murmured. "Oh God, what *have* I done?"

16

The moment he saw them, Simon Droy scurried into the toilet and slammed the door shut. This, he discovered as a couple of the phantasms slipped through the crack beneath the door, was an appalling mistake.

Finding their victim alone and trapped, they wailed and screamed and cackled with hideous laughter. Their bodies – now as wispy as mist, now as solid as stone – changed with every passing second. Long misty fingers, tipped with savage talons, scraped down his face. He raised his arms protectively, only to have razor-sharp teeth, strung out with strands of glistening drool, biting into them.

"*Aaargh*!" Simon screamed. "What's going on? What do you want from me?"

"Not *from* you, but *of* you," one of the phantasms said.

Simon turned and fumbled desperately with the handle on the door.

The second phantasm screeched with amusement as it wound itself round and round Simon's body and snapped at his exposed hand. "There's no escape," it whispered. Its body flickered and flashed like flames. "There's no way out of this. Ever."

Outside in the carriage itself, the others were faring no better. Miss Grange was pressed up against the door at the back of the buffet car, quivering with fear. Maria Fernandez was cowering in the corner of her seat, suitcase raised to fend off her attackers. Greg was climbing back over the seats and tables, retreating from the taunting, giggling phantasms which brandished clubs and pitchforks. Mandy was struggling in the grip of a trio of hefty spirits who stretched her this way, that way, till her muscles bulged, her spine cricked and her whole body cried out to be left alone.

"Go away," Miss Grange whimpered. "Please, go away."

"Oh, no," came the deep, gurgling reply. "Never ever," it breathed, and the face, swollen and waxen, twisted round into a scornful sneer. "Don't you know *anything*?"

"Know?" she said.

"Such innocence," the puffy-faced phantasm's angular blue companion chuckled. It dug Miss Grange in the ribs as if the pair of them were sharing some great joke. "Priceless!" it said, and jabbed at her again. And again. Each of the bony blows was more painful than the last.

"Stop it!" Miss Grange pleaded. "You're hurting me."

"My pleasure," replied the phantasm, and hurt her all the more.

Miss Grange looked round the carriage. "Help!" she cried out weakly. "Help!" But her pleas fell on deaf ears.

There were seven people in the carriage – eight including Nick (who had still not emerged from the buffet-bar behind the steel roller). Perhaps if they had all worked together they might have repelled the phantasms – by rational if not physical means. After all, ghosts, ghouls and evil spirits, they had all agreed, were a product of a feverish imagination. They had no place in reality.

Yet working together was never an option. At no point did the situation become one of *us versus them*. The phantasms would not allow it. Instead, like pack-animals, they hunted in twos and threes, picking their victims off one by one and growing stronger as they did so.

"For God's sake, let go of me!" Mandy Hurley screamed as the increasingly corporeal phantasms continued to wrench violently at her body, twisting her into positions no person should ever be in. It felt as though her entire body was being wrenched out of shape. She didn't know how much more she could take.

"I thought you liked exercise!" one of the phantasms leered, and all three of them laughed unpleasantly.

"Enough," Mandy pleaded. "Enough…"

"You will never have enough!" they screeched in unison. "Never!"

All at once, the lights flickered and the carriage was plunged into darkness. Greg Tolson, his back turned against his attackers, stared out through the window in absolute disbelief. For a moment he forgot all about the blows raining down on him.

"Where on earth are we?" he gasped. He stared open-mouthed at the smoking craters, the jagged peaks, the rocky plateaus. "This can't be happening," he reasoned. "I don't believe it. I don't believe *any* of it…"

"Then believe this!" came a strident voice, and a blinding pain shot through his body as something sharp jabbed viciously into his back.

The lights came back on. The landscape faded. Greg spun round to meet his tormentors face to face.

They sneered and spat. Forked tongues tasted the scorched air.

"No, no!" Greg gasped, struggling hard against the rising hysteria bubbling up in his throat. "I still don't believe it. Not this..."

At that moment, the intercom crackled into action. A man's voice emerged, nasal, gushing.

"*Network Railways wish to apologize for any inconvenience*," it said earnestly.

Greg snorted. "This is all some kind of a joke," he muttered. He stared at the phantasms with their curly horns and their cloven hoofs. One of them stabbed at him savagely with its pitchfork.

"Joke?" it said. "The joke is on you."

"*Network Railways wish to apologize for any inconvenience*," the earnest announcer said again.

Maria Fernandez quaked with fear. She had pushed herself as far as she could into the corner of the seat with her fingers in her ears and her eyes screwed tightly shut – but there was nothing she could do to escape the attention of the terrifying creatures.

They danced around her, plucking at her clothing and pinching the ample figure it concealed. They poked at her ears. They pulled her hair. One of them grabbed hold of the heavy gold chain around her neck and yanked it back so violently that she thought she would black out.

But no such luck. There was no escape as the gleeful phantasms continued to torment her.

For a third time, the nasal voice gushed its apology over the intercom, the repetition undercutting its sincerity. It was clearly just a taped message recorded for every eventuality. Discomfort. Disorder. Delay.

Cowering down beneath a table, Darren and Vicky were warding off the attacks as best they could. "Bet they never thought they'd ever be apologizing for this," said Darren humourlessly.

Vicky shook her head. Bone-scraping terror racked her body. "I... I can't believe what's happening. It's..." She fell silent. No words could express her feelings as the scene unfolded around her.

The evil spirits – previously so insubstantial – were now all as solid as their victims and infinitely more terrible. Sounds of horror and pain echoed round the carriage. Pinched and punched, scratched and stabbed, the passengers were suffering. Miss Grange and Mandy howled. Maria Fernandez whimpered. Greg screamed with rage and frustration. While the demons themselves, urged on by the responses of those they were tormenting, were working themselves up into a frenzy.

They ripped out the seats, slashing at the upholstery and pulling out the stuffing. They tore down the luggage racks. They etched their names in the window glass.

"Azdrigal woz 'ere," Darren muttered in disbelief. He clung tighter to Vicky. "*Is* all this some kind of joke? A hoax? Do you think there are hidden cameras?"

Just then, three of the demons raced back towards them. Their eyes blazed. Their pitchforks glinted.

"Wh... What?" Vicky stammered. She could feel the heat emanating from their bodies; smell the mix of rotting and sulphur on their breath...

"Welcome to the fright train!" one of them screeched and, cackling with laughter, they all darted away.

Vicky turned towards Darren and held him tightly. "What did it mean?" she said.

"I... I don't know," Darren replied shakily. "Get off!" he bellowed, as one of the demons leapt on to his back and sank its teeth into his shoulder. "Get off!"

Kicking aside the creatures scrabbling around her own legs, Vicky reached up, tore the grinning demon from Darren's back and hurled it away.

"*Network Railways wish to apologize for any inconvenience*," the voice assured them once again.

The demon landed and sprang round, teeth bared. Others joined it. Hissing and spitting with rage, they advanced on the terrified couple.

At the same time, the toilet door behind them

burst open and Simon rushed out, face white and dripping with sweat, and stumbled off down the lurching aisle.

"Oh, no you don't!" screeched one of the demons as it did a flying somersault through the air and landed at Simon's feet. It pointed an accusing finger. "Naughty, naughty," it said.

Simon spun round, only to find himself confronted with the other demons, grinning maniacally. The larger of the two was carrying a branding iron which glowed white hot.

"No!" Simon squealed. "NO!"

Sniggering with delight, the demon lunged forwards. The glowing metal grazed his shirt, and filled the carriage with the smell of scorched material. Simon staggered backwards. The demon lunged again.

Vicky closed her eyes and clamped her hands over her ears. "I just can't bear it!" she wailed. "It's not..." The words stuck in her throat.

Darren gripped Vicky's shoulders. "What *are* they?" he muttered.

It was the question that Vicky had been asking herself over and over. This wasn't down to the shock of the crash or the heat in the carriage. She kept remembering what Darren had said: "*...or the carriage is possessed*".

But surely it wasn't possible. Ghosts and ghouls simply don't exist. Everyone knows that.

Yet the demons are so damned real! Look at their teeth and claws; listen to the way they squeal!

"Well?" said Darren.

"I..." She hesitated.

"Tell me," said Darren.

She shook her head, trying hard to stop the burning tears from welling up in her eyes. "The carriage," she said. "I think it *must* be possessed."

As they hung in the air, the words sounded crazy. Yet Darren was not laughing. "Me too," he said softly.

Vicky sniffed as the tears trickled over, and ran down her cheek. "But what could have happened that could attract such ... such evil?" she said.

"Leave me, leave me, leave me," pleaded Miss Grange.

"Something bad," said Darren, his voice low and trembling. "Something very bad. Murder. Mass murder..."

"But the carriage is new," said Vicky. "We'd have seen it on the news if..."

"I don't know," said Darren. "Maybe something happened when the carriage was being manufactured. Some kind of factory accident. I... Oh God!" he shrieked.

The three demons were back, hurtling towards them from three different angles. Their eyes flashed red; their slavering mouths gaped.

Darren gasped. He'd never seen such utter,

all-consuming wickedness in a face before. He grabbed a suitcase lying nearby, swung it round and smashed it into the first of the advancing demons.

At the same moment, the second demon launched itself off the floor and flew, claws outstretched, straight at Vicky's face. She froze, unable either to leap aside or raise her arms for protection. The demon bared its teeth. Still Vicky could not move a muscle. Eyes unblinking, she stared at the glinting claws as they got closer, closer.

This is it, she thought.

"Get off! Get away!" Darren yelled as he swung the suitcase a second time. The blow sent the demon tumbling back through the air, followed a moment later by the third. "And leave us alone!"

All three demons jumped back on to their feet and hunkered down. They mewled with amusement. Their eyes flashed with malice.

"Leave you alone?" they screamed. "Leave *you*? Alone?"

"Yeah," said Vicky, finding her voice at last. "Whatever happened in the past, it's nothing to do with us. Any of us."

The demon scratched its belly with its claws, threw back its head and roared with scornful laughter. The two others joined in.

"That's what they all say!" one of them cried out triumphantly.

"What? What?" Vicky and Darren demanded.

But the other two were no longer listening. As the body of Maria Fernandez slumped down on to the floor before them, they turned and leapt upon her. One of them jabbed its pitchfork into her legs. One of them bit her neck.

Vicky quaked with horror. She turned away, but the scene was being repeated everywhere she looked in the runaway carriage. The passengers were being taunted and tortured by the evil demons, their terrified cries drowned out by their tormentors' howls of malevolent laughter. There was nowhere to run to, nowhere to hide.

Greg was pinned up against the buffet-bar. Mandy and Simon were cowering under a table, trying their best to fend off their attackers. Miss Grange was on one of the benches, curled up into a tiny ball. She was not moving.

And all round them were the demons, malice etched into their wrinkled red faces. They whooped and jeered as they hopped about their hapless victims. The battle was all but over. Suddenly they turned on Vicky herself once again, gurning maniacally and stabbing at her menacingly with their sharp weapons.

"Darren!" she wailed. "Watch out! They're coming back!"

But Darren seemed unaware of what was going on. He was staring at the far end of the carriage.

"Darren!" Vicky cried. She turned round and followed the line of his gaze.

"Infernal and eternal," the demons were goading as they danced closer. "Eternal and infernal."

"The door," Darren gasped.

As he spoke, Nick emerged, a piece of paper clutched in his bony hands. He looked neat and well-groomed: not at all like someone who, only moments before, had been in the middle of uncontrollable rage.

A look of confusion passed momentarily over his face, followed by a spasm of rage as he surveyed the scene. His face darkened, his eyes blazed, his thin lips parted.

"WHAT IN HELL'S NAME IS THE MEANING OF THIS?" he roared.

17

At the sound of the monstrous voice, everyone – human and demon alike – froze. Nick kicked the door shut. All eyes followed him as he stepped forwards.

The demons watched him warily as he picked his way among the debris, as sure-footed as a goat. His head was raised. His eyes glinted with fire. Those he brushed past shrunk back fearfully.

"What do you think you're doing?" he said, his voice low and soothing. "This is not yet the time." The demons looked away, shame-faced, mute. "WELL?" he bellowed.

"The door was open," came a voice from over near the window.

"You never, *ever* board the train," he shouted.

"You should know that. How dare you be so impatient! Procedure must be followed!" His eyes sparked. "Sulphurous pits!" he exclaimed. "You have a whole eternity ahead of you!"

"We didn't think..." murmured a voice, close by him.

Nick spun round and lashed out savagely at the demon who had been foolish enough to speak unbidden. The creature squealed with pain as it hurtled across the carriage.

"That's just it!" Nick roared. "You didn't think!" And he began laying into the demons, kicking them, cuffing them, sending them scurrying for cover. "Insolent! Ignorant! Imbecilic!" he ranted, punctuating each fresh insult with a blow from his fist or foot. The demons cringed and cowered and cried out with pain.

Vicky trembled and grabbed hold of Darren's arm fearfully. She looked at the terrified demons, at the cowering passengers, and at the buffet steward himself. He was lost in a frenzy of raging violence. No wonder Greg and Simon had been so alarmed earlier.

"W... Who is he?" she whispered.

"I don't know," said Darren, shaking his head. He knew who it *looked* like, but no, it was impossible. Surely.

The train gave a sudden lurch as it continued at full tilt down the sloping tracks. Darren and Vicky fell back into their seat. Miss Grange – who had just come round – rolled heavily down on to the floor and cried out. Nick spun round.

"My dear lady," he said, extending a bony hand. His fury had quite disappeared. He helped her to her seat. "There is something I need to discuss," he said amiably, and waved the sheet of paper around. "That all of us need to discuss," he added.

The squatting demons gabbled to one another and glanced up at him apprehensively.

"Not you!" Nick said sharply. "I'll deal with you later."

The demons looked round, puzzled.

"BE GONE!" he roared, and clapped his hands together.

There was a flurry of movement and, as Vicky and Darren watched, the demons began to break up, to lose their solidity, to return to the swirling phantasms from which they had been formed.

Nick raised his arms. "NOW!" he bellowed.

For a moment, the inside of the speeding carriage wailed and whistled with the sound of the dusty twisters as they flew through the air, searching for a way out. Then, one by one, they disappeared into the air-conditioning grilles in the ceiling, hissing as they did so. Outside at last, they hovered by the windows for a moment, before spinning off and away into shadowy landscape. Finally the last one was gone. The carriage seemed curiously empty.

Vicky sighed nervously. The others picked themselves weakly up off the floor. Their faces were grey with fear, their hands trembled, their eyes darted round anxiously like the eyes of frightened horses. Nick leant back against the counter of the closed buffet and surveyed them, eyebrows raised and a smirk playing over his lips.

"You poor souls," he said softly. "Sit down over there," he said, pointing to the curved benches in the snack-and-chat area. "There's less mess there." He beckoned to Darren and Vicky. "Come and sit with the others."

Vicky swallowed anxiously, bewildered by Nick's mood swings yet relieved that he had made the demons leave. She climbed to her feet. Darren followed her. The train hurtled on faster than ever, ominously rattling and clunking as the nervous pair made their way back through the devastation of the railway carriage.

Nick turned back to the others. He raised the piece of paper high. Vicky noticed the two angry-looking red marks high up on his forehead, one on each side.

"You will be pleased to know that I have finally managed to locate the list I was looking for," he said, smiling pleasantly. "If you would all have your vouchers ready."

The passengers stared back at Nick dumbly. How could he be so calm in the face of what had just happened? they asked themselves. Why was he not as terrified as them?

"Chop-chop!" said Nick, clapping his hands together.

Obediently, they all set off to the end of the train. Only Miss Grange held back. "But what about...?" she began.

"Yes, yes," said Nick. "Just sit yourself down with the others. Everything will soon be revealed."

The others were seated around the semi–circular bench when Vicky and Darren arrived, Simon Droy at one end, and Miss Grange at the other. They squeezed in next to the old woman and looked up at Nick expectantly.

"The list," he said, raising it high and looking from person to person. "It had slipped behind the drinks dispenser. As soon as I've checked your vouchers against the names, I'll see to those refreshments I know you're all dying to have."

Greg shook his head in amazement. "You're talking about refreshments," he said. "After all we've been through!"

"Forgive me, sir. I thought you were thirsty," said Nick, his gaze hardening menacingly.

"I... I am," said Greg. "But..."

"Then kindly don't interrupt," said Nick. He turned his head to the right and nodded towards the person at the end of the line. "Your voucher," he said.

With shaking fingers, Simon pulled the red voucher from his pocket and handed it over. For a moment, Nick scanned the list. Then, with a smile, he put a tick next to a name. "Simon James Droy," he said, and looked up. "Well?"

Simon glanced round at the others. "I'll have a bottle of orange juice, a bacon sandwich – and a gin and tonic. A *large* gin and tonic."

Nick beamed. "Is there anything else you want to say ... to ask ... any other weakness you'd like to confess to?"

"Go on, then," said Simon. "I'll have a doughnut."

"Very good," said Nick. "But that wasn't quite what I had in mind."

Simon frowned.

"First of all, you must know why you are here." He smiled. "It is the procedure."

"I don't understand," said Simon, puzzled.

Nick leant forwards, his elbows resting on his knees. "I rather thought you'd want to ask about the fire," he said, the smile disappearing from his lips. "You do remember the fire, don't you?"

The others listened in open-mouthed silence.

"Y... Yes," Simon replied, shocked to discover that the steward also knew about it.

"And weren't you curious?"

Maria Fernandez leaned forward. "You mean you know what truly happened?" she said.

Nick looked round at the faces of the seven shaken individuals. The pleasant mask had slipped away to reveal the evil face beneath. The eyes blazed, cruel and hard. The face darkened.

"I know everything," he screeched. Sharp teeth glinted as he threw back his head and roared with terrible laughter. "*Everything*!"

18

"Remain seated!" Nick bellowed as Greg went to jump up. He pulled himself up to his full height. His teeth glistened; his eyes glowed red. The red marks on his forehead had turned to two boil-like bumps. He thrust his goatee beard forwards, "Now!"

Greg shrank back. He couldn't confront the man a second time. Not now. Not after everything he'd seen and heard. And, save for the involuntary trembling which gripped their bodies, none of the others made a move either.

The carriage rattled on faster than ever, if that was possible, full-tilt down the ever steepening track. And all the while, it grew hotter, and hotter, and hotter. The air smelled of smouldering electrics, scorched cloth, sulphur. It burned the sensitive skin inside the noses of the petrified passengers; it stung their fear-struck eyes.

"You!" Nick screamed, as he spun round and pointed a yellow-taloned finger at Simon Droy. Simon cowered. Nick rubbed his hands together gleefully. "Murdered him, didn't you?" he said. "That nightwatchman."

"No. I... I..." Simon stammered.

"You had him burned alive. And now it is your turn!" he shrieked. "You will burn in those bowels of fiery hell you already seem to know so much about – for ever!"

The others stared at one another in horror. What was he talking about? Could this be...? Were they...? No one dared put words to their worst fears.

"Next!" said Nick. "You!"

Mandy meekly held out her voucher. Nick snatched it away, consulted his list and made a tick.

"Amanda Hurley," he read off. "Twenty-three years old." He looked up, his eyes glinting malevolently. "More avarice! More murder! How tediously predictable you all are!" he said, and roared with laughter again.

Mandy clamped her hands over her ears and hummed as loud as she could. Nick's expression turned as hard as stone. His skin reddened; his pupils thinned to two vertical lines. He stepped forward and tore away her hands.

"Pushing illegal drugs on minors," he cried out gleefully.

The others gasped.

"But, it wasn't like that," Mandy protested. "They weren't proper drugs. I mean, not like crack, or heroin..."

"Priceless! Priceless!" Nick cried, laughing all the louder. "Do you know what the post-mortem discovered?"

Mandy fell still. She felt again those bony fingers gripping her heart. Her breath came in short, sharp gasps.

"*Do* you?" he bellowed, his face contorted with malicious amusement. "In amongst the lethal cocktail of drugs was one intended only for use on cattle." He laughed contemptuously. "Cattle! No wonder they died."

"I... I..."

But Nick was no longer paying her any attention. Time, as he was only too aware, was running out. "You," he said to the next in the row.

Greg looked up. "I can't find my voucher," he said sullenly.

Nick stepped forwards furiously. He pulled Greg roughly to his feet by his shirt collar, removed the slip of paper from his back pocket and shoved him back. He held up the voucher against the list.

"Gregory Miles Montegue-Tolson," he announced.

"A man after my own heart by the look of things!"

"No, you've got it all wrong!" said Greg. "It was suicide, not murder. "I never..."

Nick glanced at the window impatiently. Vicky followed his gaze. Outside, the flickering darkness smeared past the windows, filling her with nameless horror.

"I really don't have the time for this," Nick snapped. "You taunted him, you intimidated him, you belittled and humiliated him. In front of his colleagues. In front of his family..."

"No," Greg protested.

"You bullied and bullied him until he was a nervous wreck. You drove him to suicide," he said, hissing with gleeful amusement. "I couldn't have done better myself."

"A person should be responsible for his or her own actions," Greg said, repeating his own self-justification.

"I couldn't agree more!" said Nick triumphantly. "You might as well have drawn the blade across his wrists yourself. You *are* responsible. Next!"

He leaned forwards and snatched the next voucher. "Señora Maria Luisa Caruso Fernandez. Wife of Colonel Augusto Felipe Fernandez," he said, and his tongue – black and forked – flicked round his lips. "Someone I look forward to meeting ... in due course."

"You?" she said, her heart pounding so hard, she

feared it would burst. "Meet Augusto? Wh... Who are you?"

"Can you not guess?" said Nick, slicking back his hair to reveal two small horns, jutting up from the top of his forehead. He pressed his blood-red face into hers. "But you are not here because of the bloody army coup, or the stadium massacre, or the torture and execution of the missing ones, as I'm sure you know. But rather, because of Rosa Vicario. The woman your husband raped every night..."

"No," gasped Maria Fernandez. The others shrunk away from her.

"The woman you had locked away and tortured!" Nick shouted.

"No ... it was..."

"The woman you condemned to death!" He raised his taloned hands and covered his face. His shoulders shook. For a moment it looked as if he was sobbing, overwhelmed by the burden of knowledge he had to bear.

He looked up. There were tears streaming down his face. Tears of laughter. Tears of delight.

"You concocted a pack of lies to seal her fate," he screamed, "thereby sealing your own!"

"Are you saying that everyone in this carriage is a murderer?" said Simon weakly.

"Seven of a kind!" Nick shrieked. "And now you all belong to me!" He turned to Miss Grange. "Next!"

Vicky felt her insides churning. She looked at Nick; at his red face, his goat-like face, the two gleaming horns. How could this be happening?

"But I haven't killed anyone," she protested. "I haven't!"

"Me neither," said Darren.

Nick ignored them. "Give it to me!" he demanded, as he tore the voucher from Miss Grange's trembling fingers. As he did so, there was a sudden stomach-wrenching lurch, and the carriage abruptly pitched forwards. Luggage, rubbish and pieces of debris skittered to the front of the train.

Screaming with fear, everyone grabbed on to the handrails, the tables, each other.

Nick scanned the list calmly. The faster the ride and hotter the air, the more he seemed to grow, both in strength and stature.

"Evelyn Maud Grange. Spinster. Retired nurse. Sixty-eight years old," he rattled off, apparently unaware that the carriage was now hurtling downwards so fast it felt as though it had left the tracks and was dropping through space.

"No," Miss Grange gasped. She was down on her knees, clinging on desperately to the sharply sloping table. "I admit it, but ... she ... she was old. She was in pain."

"She was in your care!" said Nick, and burst into laughter. "Oh, how I do love all this," he said. "If only I hadn't wasted so much time looking for the damned list." He chuckled. "Or should that be the list of the damned?"

Just then, there was a violent jolt that shook the entire carriage. Miss Grange screamed. Simon Droy grunted with pain as his head slammed back against the luggage rack. The sound of screeching metal on metal filled the air. A shower of glittering sparks flew back past the window.

"Sadly, as I said, time is the one thing we do not have," said Nick. "We are approaching our destination. Next!"

"But it was all intended for the best," Miss Grange protested. "I..."

Nick turned on her. "You played God!" he bellowed. "And for that, you shall dance with the devil for eternity!" He looked back at Vicky. "Give me your voucher!"

Vicky froze as he strutted towards her, his blazing red eyes boring into her skull. She could smell the stench of decay on his breath.

"The voucher!" he screeched.

"I... I..." she whimpered tremulously, and shook her head. Scalding tears poured down her cheeks. "I haven't got one."

"M... Me neither," said Darren.

"Don't lie to me!" Nick roared. He inspected his list. "There are two names left on my list. One a man's. One a woman's. He thrust his arm out at Darren. "Barry Vincent Cooper," he said.

"No," said Darren.

"Twenty-two years old. And you," he said, swinging round and pointing at Vicky. "Michelle Crawford."

"I'm not, Vicky screamed back. "I'm Vicky. Vicky Amis."

"Don't try and deny it!" Nick shouted. "It's here in red and white."

The locked wheels squealed like wildcats. The sparks flew past the windows in a shower of fiery orange.

"Two joyriders!" Nick continued, louder than ever. "You stole a car, didn't you?"

"No, no, no," said Vicky.

"Taking it in turns to drive. You killed an old man," he shouted at Darren. "To prove how tough you were. And you..."

"You've got the wrong people," said Vicky.

"You crashed into a crossing patrol. Eight people died. The crossing-man. Two mothers and five young children." He roared with laughter as he looked along the row of terrified faces. "Scum, the lot of you," he cackled maliciously, and rubbed his scaly hands together with glee. "But Michelle, here, came top of the class!"

"I am not Michelle!" said Vicky defiantly. She

began fumbling in her pocket. "Here. Here," she said, pulling out two folded pieces of paper. "I can prove it."

Nick hesitated for a moment. "What are they?" he said.

"My birth certificate," she said. "See, Victoria Louisa Amis. And here," she said, fumbling to open the second one, "Darren's one."

"What the...?" Darren exclaimed, wondering why Vicky should be carrying his birth certificate.

"Convenient," said Nick suspiciously. "A little too convenient."

"It was meant to be a surprise," said Vicky. "Silly, I know, but ... I was going to propose. You…" she looked down tearfully, "you need birth certificates to get married..."

"Then where are Barry Cooper and Michelle..." He glanced back at the list. "Michelle Crawford?"

Vicky and Darren looked at each other. "Shel and Baz," they said in unison.

"We saw them," said Darren, turning back to Nick. "At the station."

"They must have missed the train," Vicky added.

For a moment, Nick fell still. His eyes glowered. "It can't be," he said, his voice a low growl. "It isn't possible. No! NO!"

Growing louder in his mounting agitation, Nick whipped himself up into a fury. His eyes blazed. The veins at his temples pulsed. He screwed the birth certificates up into two tiny balls and tossed them aside.

"This is outrageous!" he screamed. "Mistakes will not be tolerated!"

The screeching of the brakes intensified as the train continued to slow down. Outside the window, silhouetted against a bank of flames, were the demons, back once more and pawing at the glass with renewed vigour. Howling. Jeering. Spitting.

Consumed with rage, Nick ripped at his clothes and kicked off his shoes as he paced up and down, lashing out viciously, muttering under his breath.

Vicky stared in horror.

The goat's eyes. The forked tongue. The horns.

She trembled with disbelief.

The chest, bare now, was as red as the grimacing face. Where his feet should have been, there were instead two cloven hoofs. And as he strutted furiously back and forth, a scaly tail with an arrowhead tip swished backwards and forwards.

Powerful. Imposing. Evil. The transformation was complete. Nick, the solicitous buffet steward, had finally revealed who he really was.

Struck dumb with terror, Vicky turned away. She felt Darren clutching hold of her arm, and heard him speak.

"What is going to happen to us?" he whispered.

The Devil stopped pacing, spun round and thrust its great horned head towards him. "Happen?" it roared, its teeth glinting in the fiery glow. "You're about to find out!"

19

"**R**ight," the Devil said, its goat-like eyes narrowed in thought. It spun round to address the cowering group of passengers huddled together at the back of the train. "Away from that door, you lot!"

The people looked at one another and shuffled about indecisively.

"Come on!" it commanded, its voice striking fear into each and every one of them. "We must act quickly." It paused. "And lest there be any further misunderstanding, I am talking to Simon Droy, Amanda Hurley, Greg Tolson, Evelyn Grange and Maria Fernandez. Jump to it!"

Rigid with fear, no one moved.

"Did you not hear me?" it bellowed, strutting

forwards on its heavy cloven hoofs. "Do you dare to defy your new master? Go! Go now!" It turned round and looked Vicky and Darren up and down, and scowled. "While I deal with these two."

Relieved to discover that the main focus of attention had apparently shifted from them, the five hapless passengers slowly began to pick their way down to the front of the carriage.

"Hurry up!" the Devil roared impatiently.

Like a small flock of frightened sheep with a dog snapping at their heels, Simon, Mandy and Greg scurried off down the sloping aisle, with Maria Fernandez close behind them. Miss Grange paused to look round. "My bag," she said. "I can't find my bag."

"Your bag!" the Devil exclaimed, and the carriage resounded with the sound of scornful laughter. At the windows, the demons pressed their sneering, snarling faces against the glass. "Do you seriously think you will be taking anything with you where you're going? Do you?" it roared.

"It's ... it's got lots of useful things in it," she said.

"Everything you need will be provided," it said, laughing all the louder. Then, strutting towards her, it grasped her by the shoulders.

Sparks leapt up into the air; Miss Grange screamed with pain.

"You will obey!" the Devil screeched as it spun

her forcefully round and propelled her down the aisle in the direction of the others.

Vicky gasped. Where the beast's taloned hands had gripped, Miss Grange's clothes were scorched and smoking. Grinning maliciously, it turned on her and Darren again.

"Now for the intruders!" he hissed.

Intruders? The word sent a chill down Vicky's back. It made it sound as though they had gatecrashed the terrible events on purpose. It wasn't their fault they'd ended up in the buffet car in place of Shel and Baz.

"No one is to board this train save for those expressly summoned," the Devil told them severely. "You have broken every regulation in the book." It turned and spat out a black ball of phlegm that burned into the carpet where it landed. The demons at the windows gurned with malice and scratched furiously at the glass. "I've a good mind..."

"But we're not to blame," Vicky said desperately. "We only came in here because the rest of the train was full."

"The door should have been locked!" said the Devil.

"But it wasn't," said Darren.

"You shouldn't be here," the Devil persisted.

"Exactly!" Vicky cried. "We're not on your list... You've made a mistake... It's all *your* fault!"

The moment she spoke, Vicky knew she had gone too far. The Devil's red face turned purple with rage. It threw its head back and screeched with rage, its cloven feet pawing at the ground.

"Get over there!" it bellowed. "By the door!"

Tentatively, Darren made a move towards the aisle.

"Not *that* door!" it shrieked. It turned and pointed to the emergency exit at the back of the train. "That door!"

For a moment, they hesitated.

"I'm warning you," the Devil snarled.

Taking each other by the hand, Vicky and Darren did as they had been told. They climbed the steeply sloping snack-and-chat area and on past the steel roller of the buffet which had never opened. The train juddered as the brakes continued to bite. Darren reached out for the fire hydrant on the wall and held on.

They both looked back.

"Open the door, then," said the Devil.

"The door?" said Vicky. Although slower, the train was still rattling along far too fast to risk jumping out. "But we can't. It's too dangerous. We'll be killed!"

The Devil's jaw dropped in surprise. The next instant, its face twisted up with gleeful malice. It cackled with hideous laughter, it shook its head, it slapped its sides. "Killed?" it spluttered. "Killed? You ridiculous creature! You're already dead!"

The words fell on her ears like a hammer blow. She felt giddy. Bile filled her mouth. She clung tightly on to Darren's arm.

Dead? But...

She glanced at the frightened group at the other end of the carriage, and found them staring back at her, terror in their eyes. They looked so small, so insignificant. Five ordinary people, yet each one with a guilty secret in their past – a past that they were now paying for.

"But we haven't done anything," said Vicky. "I mean, nothing really bad..."

"Then open the door and leave!" screamed the Devil. "There'll be hell to pay if you don't!"

Darren turned and, as the train lurched and jolted, he reached out for the handle with his free hand.

"GO!"

The Devil lowered its arm and pointed at the handle. A fizzing blue bolt of electricity hissed through the air. As it struck, the door burst open and slammed back against the wall.

For a moment Vicky and Darren remained still, staring ahead in horror at the flickering darkness outside. The next, they cried out as a sudden blast of scorching air wrapped itself around them and sucked them from the train.

"NO!" they screamed, as they tumbled away from the swiftly departing carriage.

"Till next time!" the Devil roared, and the air trembled with the sound of its demonic laughter.

There was a loud bang as the carriage door slammed shut.

Everything fell silent.

Falling. They were falling down, down, down... Or were they rising?

Far, far below them the dim glow of yellow light was abruptly extinguished as the carriage spun out of view.

Yes, perhaps they *were* rising. Or perhaps they were simply floating in one place, while all about them the dark, flickering air was rushing past. It was hard to tell.

Above and below them the darkness stretched away in a neverending twisting tunnel. There was no end in sight, whichever way they were falling – nothing at all but the blur of darkness as the air rushed past.

"Hold tight!" Darren cried.

Vicky squeezed his hand. "You, too!" she said.

Then, all at once, everything changed. Through the wisps of sulphurous mist they saw the blackened stones and molten rock they had seen through the carriage windows. The pungent air glowed blood-red. It was like falling into the crater of a vast, active volcano.

Below them was a spot of light. Or was it above

them? Either way, it was getting closer with every passing second.

Bigger. Brighter....

Both Vicky and Darren screwed their eyes shut and shielded them with their free hands. Yet the light was so intense that even this could not keep it from dazzling them. It shimmered and hummed, filling their eyes and ears and flooding through their pores until both of them were aglow with pure white light.

"Vicky!" shouted Darren.

"Darren!" Vicky shouted back. "Darren!"

"Dar..." Vicky went to shout again, and cried out as a spasm of pain shot through her chest.

She looked round nervously. It was dark. Beams of yellow light darted round in the cold, night air. For a brief second, section after section of the twisted wreckage was illuminated – buckled panels, crushed seats, a mangled steel roller – before the light bounced away. And there were voices; urgent, troubled voices.

"Darren?" she whispered, her voice low and husky. "Darren, where are you?"

She tried to move, but the tangle of metal was pinning her to the ground, and the attempt made her cry out all the louder.

"Vicky?" she heard.

"Darren. I'm here."

"Are you all right?"

"My chest ... it hurts to breathe," she said.

"Whatever you do," said Darren, "don't move."

Vicky smiled. "Can't," she whispered, and another sharp pain jarred through her chest.

"Neither can I," said Darren. "Help!" he shouted. "*Help!*"

All at once there was activity around them. The beams of light focused in on them, illuminating the destruction brightly. There was hope in the voices now.

"It came from this way," said one.

"Mind where you're putting your feet. The whole lot could collapse at any moment."

"Help!" Darren called a third time, and he pushed his arm up through the twisted lengths of metal. "Over here!"

"There's his hand," said the first voice, and Darren looked up to see the torchlight shining straight into his eyes. "We'll soon get you out of there, mate," he said. "Are you all right?"

"Yes, I'm OK," he said. "But my girlfriend. Vicky. She's somewhere close. I heard her. You've got to find her. She's hurt – maybe badly..."

"It's all right, mate," said the man. "Don't you worry. We'll see to her."

"She's here," shouted the second man.

"Vicky!" Darren shouted. He looked up at the man impatiently. He seemed to be taking for ever to remove the debris that was holding him down. He had his hands gripped round a buckled length of luggage rack and was pulling with all his strength.

"Nearly there," he grunted.

Darren twisted round and kicked against it with his heavy boots. With a soft creak, the metal abruptly shifted. He scrambled to his feet and staggered over the wreckage. Losing his balance, he stumbled and slipped. He clung on to the back of a broken seat for support and glanced round. A policeman was standing at the foot of the bank the carriage had rolled down. Beside him was a row of stretchers.

Darren shuddered. There were bodies on five of them, each one covered up with a blanket.

He turned away and continued to the spot where the second man was kneeling. He crouched down, taking care not to disturb the precariously balanced jumble of debris, and there below him, he saw Vicky's face looking up at him from the shadows underneath the crumpled metal.

"The paramedic's on his way," he said gently. "They'll have you out of here in no time."

Vicky blinked and shivered. "We crashed," she whispered. "Darren, the train crashed! We could have died..."

Darren nodded tearfully. "I know," he said. The sight of the covered bodies on the stretchers was all too fresh in his mind. "But we didn't die, Vicky. We survived. It's going to be all right now. We're alive! You and me, Vicky, we're both alive!"

20

Both Darren and Vicky were kept in hospital overnight. Darren had various cuts and bruises, but was otherwise unscathed. Vicky had two cracked ribs. Both of them were suffering from shock. Yet despite their four-hour ordeal and the noise in the wards, the pair of them slept soundly.

After breakfast the following morning, Darren was told he could leave. He put on his clothes, made his way to Vicky's ward and found her, dressed and seated in the chair next to her bed, her nose buried in a newspaper.

"Hiya!" he said.

She looked up. "Hiya, Darren." They kissed. "I'm just waiting for the doctor to see me, then I can go. She folded the paper and nodded at the headline.

FIVE DEAD IN RAIL CRASH.

"Did you see this? Apparently, it was caused by a signal failure." She found a paragraph with her finger and read out, "A southbound local train ploughed into the buffet car of the Scotland Express at 18.42..."

Darren nodded. "We were so lucky!" he said.

"You can say that again," said Vicky. "I... I was just reading about the ones who died," she said, and flicked back to the middle of the paper. "Apparently one of them was the wife of that dictator Elena's always going on about. Augusto Fernandez. We went on that march."

"It must have been that woman in the fur coat," said Darren. "Do you remember? The Ocelot."

"Yes," said Vicky.

"And the others?"

"Errm... Greg Tolson, a businessman. That must have been Action Man. Amanda Hurley, some kind of a model. The Starlet. Simon Droy, an 'entrepreneur' – whatever that means..."

"The Spiv," said Darren. "The one with the mobile."

"And Evelyn Grange." Vicky smiled ruefully. "A retired nurse."

"Matron," said Darren softly.

Vicky's eyes filled with tears. "Oh Darren," she

sobbed. "There we were giving them nicknames, taking the mickey and now ... now they're all dead..."

Darren stooped down next to the chair and hugged her gently. "It's a miracle that we survived," he said. Vicky sniffed, and he felt her nodding. "And you know what?"

"What?" Vicky said, her voice muffled and low.

Darren pulled away and held her by her shoulders.

"We can learn something from what happened."

"We can?"

"From now on, we're going to live every minute to the full. Life's too short – too precious – to squander a single moment."

Vicky smiled bravely and dried her eyes. "You're right," she said, and frowned.

"What is it?" said Darren.

"You'll think I'm stupid," she said, shaking her head.

"I already do," said Darren, adding hastily, "Joke!"

Vicky smiled. "It's not just about living every minute to the full," she said. "It's about treating every minute as though it could be your last." She paused. "You remember yesterday, when I shouted at those two on the platform?"

Darren nodded. "Shel and Baz," he said with a smirk.

"Well, I've decided. That sort of thing's not going to happen any more. I'm going to be much nicer from now on! To everyone." She laughed. "Even you!'

Just then, they heard the sound of someone clearing their throat and looked round. Expecting to see a doctor in a white coat, they were surprised to see a uniformed policeman standing there, hands behind his back.

"Excuse me for bothering you," he said, "but can you confirm that you are Victoria Louisa Amis and Darren Trevor Roberts?"

"Yes, yes we are," they replied.

"Then these birth certificates will be yours," said the policeman, holding up two crumpled pink forms. "They were discovered at the scene of the incident, screwed up in a ball. I don't suppose you happen to know why."

Vicky's jaw dropped. She reached round to her back pocket in disbelief. It was empty. "I... I haven't got a clue," she said. "I must have dropped them somehow..."

"What were you doing with my birth certificate anyway?" said Darren.

"I ... errm..." Vicky blushed. "It was for the surprise I told you about," she said to Darren, and turned to the policeman. "When the train crashed we were on our way up to Scotland for a fortnight's holiday," she explained, and sighed. "A cottage on a lake." She smiled. "I mean, *loch*. I'd booked a scuba-diving course for us both. You needed your birth certificate to enrol. I suppose they must have slipped out of my pocket." She frowned, puzzled. "But why would anyone screw them up?"

The policeman shrugged. "I daresay we'll never know," he said. "Still, glad to be able to return them to their rightful owners." He handed the birth certificates over. "You take care, now," he said.

"Thank you, officer," said Vicky.

"Yeah, thanks," said Darren.

The policeman smiled, turned and set off down the ward. Then, two beds away, he turned back.

"By the way," he said. "Your luggage is being held down at the station." He paused. "You really should take that holiday of yours, you know. You've only missed a couple of days. A cottage on a loch. Scuba-diving. It sounds just the job to put everything you've been through behind you."

"Yeah, maybe," said Vicky uncertainly.

"Well, I've said my piece," said the policeman, turning away again. "And you could always travel by coach."

As his heavy footsteps receded, Darren turned to Vicky. "Should we?" he said.

"Well we did agree to live every minute to the full," said Vicky. "Yes, I think we should."

"Excellent!" said Darren. "I've always wanted to go scuba-diving."

Vicky's cheeks reddened. Oh, yes," she said. "The scuba–diving..."

"What?" said Darren suspiciously. "You look guilty."

"I don't," said Vicky. She looked down and began busying herself by smoothing out the crumpled certificate with the flat of her hand.

"You are sure it was scuba–diving lessons you needed them for," Darren said.

"Of course, it was," said Vicky, brushing at a mark on the paper. "What else? I..." She paused and frowned. "Look at this," she said. "It looks scorched."

"That wouldn't surprise me," said Darren.

"But the carriage didn't catch fire," said Vicky. She held the certificate up to the light.

Darren gasped. "A hand print," he said.

"Let's see yours," said Vicky.

Darren smoothed the certificate hurriedly and held it up next to Vicky's. Though fainter, an identical hand–print had been scorched into his one, too.

"Look how long and bony the fingers are," said Vicky. "And there, the tips of the nails." She shivered. "Who do you think it was? What do you think happened?"

"I... I don't know," said Darren. "I can't remember a thing. One minute we were just sitting there waiting for the buffet to open. Then there was this almighty bang. Then, nothing – until four hours later, when I heard you crying out."

"Same here," said Vicky. "The whole thing's a complete blank."

She looked back at the two dark hand prints burnt into their birth certificates and shivered with unease. There was something deeply disturbing about them. It was as if their very lives had been touched by something destructive which, even now, cast a warning shadow over them. She folded them up and slipped them into her back pocket.

"Maybe it's better that way," she said.